Holtermann's Nugget

By the same author:

Distant Shores, 1991
The Prophet Returns, 1995
Men Over Fifty, 1997

Holtermann's Nugget

by

Gunter Schaule

INDRA PUBLISHING

Indra Publishing
PO Box 7, Briar Hill, Victoria, 3088, Australia

© Gunter Schaule, 2000.
Made and Printed in Australia by Australian Print Group.

All rights reserved.
No part of this publication may be reproduced, stored in a retrieval system, or transmitted in any form, or by any means, electronic, mechanical, photocopying, recording or otherwise, without prior written permission of the publisher.

ISBN 0 9585805 5 3

Holtermann's Nugget

To the living members of the Holterman family

Acknowledgements

With thanks and gratitude to John Holterman
for his contribution and support,
and to my wife Marianne for her collaboration and her caring.

Cover Photographs
The front and back cover photographs of Holtermann, at the Hill End blacksmiths and with the nugget, are from the Holtermann collection of the Mitchell Library, State Library of New South Wales. The photographs are used with the kind permission of the Curator of Photographs on behalf of the Library Council of New South Wales.

Contents

1885	Reunion In London	9
1860	The Hamburg Hotel, Sydney Town	21
1860	Hill End	36
1867	The All Nations Hotel	44
1868	At The Family Home	54
1869	The Hospital Tent	61
1871	Goldfields Speculators	66
1872	Reef Mining	76
1872	Endless Riches	82
1873	Sydney	94
1874	Miraculous Photographs	109
1876	Farewell From Sydney	113
1876	America	121
1877	Europe	131
1882	Parliament	137
1885	Last Birthday	148
Epilogue		163

About the Author

Gunter Schaule was born in Germany, and like his hero Bernhardt Holtermann, migrated to Australia to live a different life and make his career in a new country.

Gunter has travelled widely and maintained close friendships in all continents. He now manages his own successful business, but allows time for writing and enjoying life.

His previous books, all non-fiction, are all selling successfully internationally. *Holtermann's Nugget* is his first novel and the first of his books to be published by Indra.

Gunter lives in Sydney with his wife, Marianne.

1885

REUNION IN LONDON

Hunt was giving himself a pep talk as he walked down the elegant London street. "This is my day," he mumbled under his breath. "Today I will collect. 'Mr Edwards,' I'll say, 'I've killed Holtermann.'"

Hunt was in his fifties, with a boyish figure betrayed by an old, weathered face. In his threadbare suit he felt slightly out of place in the West End. Just back from Australia, he was aware he was walking through the hub of the British Empire, or even the pinnacle of the world for all he knew. Here Queen Victoria reigned, and here the one thousand families who formed British 'Society' had their town houses, to which they came from their vast country properties during the 'Season', when Parliament was sitting following the end of the hunt on the estates. Mr Hunt was familiar with the scenery. He had once served here as a lad. He remembered how building space was at a premium here in the most fashionable spot in the world. So much opulence had to be concentrated in the confined premises of each terrace house. Who cares what I look like, Hunt thought as he observed the hustle and bustle around him. Ladies in voluptuous, colourful long dresses and fancy hats climbing into their carriages, assisted by their footmen in powdered wigs, ornate coats, and tights showing off their well-formed legs. He saw delivery boys carrying rich provisions to the kitchens in the basements. The dining rooms would be at ground floor level. Hunt remembered glimpses he had snatched as a boy, of drawing rooms on the first floor, rooms overburdened with furnishings, heavy curtains, works of art and collectibles from around the world. Bedrooms would be located above again and servants' quarters in the roof-attic. As Hunt marveled at the varied architecture he passed, he mumbled to himself, a habit he had developed during endless work shifts alone deep down in narrow mine shafts in Australia.

"Yes, I've killed Mr Holtermann," Hunt reiterated under his breath. "Here are the newspapers from Sydney to prove he is no longer with us. Dead at forty-seven," he glowed. "A happy and exceedingly prosperous man, felled in his prime. And not even a suspicion of foul play. Your wish fulfilled, Mr Edwards. It took me many years to achieve it, but here I am to collect the agreed reward." Hunt smiled at the thought and quickened his pace. "Felled in his prime," he repeated, "the mighty Holtermann."

I don't have to tell Edwards I am not sure he was killed, Hunt schemed. But that's what Holtermann's groom had implied, anyway. He had hinted at that young governess, Victoria. She was Holtermann's mistress, he'd said, until the master got tired of her. She did him in!

Hunt felt optimistic. He savoured the warming rays of the sun on his face. His life would finally amount to something, he would have money to impress all and sundry. Who could then say he was a loser? After all those years trying his luck in the colonies, he had finally made it back to the imagined fairyland of his youth which his contorted memory had conjured up for him, where he had roamed with his mates, where he had been spoiled by his mother despite the dreadful poverty in their cramped hovel, despite the grime and the hopeless drunkenness that was their lot.

In Mr Edward's terrace house, the butler in his horizontally striped waistcoat knocked briefly and entered the drawing room on the first floor.

"Mr Edwards, Sir, your solicitor is here for his appointment with you, and another gentleman has arrived, unannounced, to see you. All the way from Australia, he says. A Mr Hunt."

Edwards put his book down with a thump as he rose quickly. "Hunt, you say! What is he doing here in England?"

"He mentioned he is planning to settle back home, as you did, Sir. But he doesn't appear to be well off, Sir, if you permit my observation."

Edwards sat down again. He adjusted his cravat. "Who can say I know that man? Yes, tell him I met many people in the years I spent in Australia, but that is long ago. Tell him I don't remember him. And say I am very busy and I don't have time to see him. Give him my regrets and send him away."

The butler stood hesitatingly and then proceeded to stir the fire. "Send him away, you said, Sir?" he repeated.

"Certainly; that's the beginning and the end of it."

"Yes, Sir, as you wish."

"I am ready to see the other gentleman now."

Edwards was fashionably attired according to the latest trend. The style was modelled after the riding and hunting costumes of the rural aristocracy and gentry, who resided a good part of the year in London. The landed gentry had not only introduced their hunting attire from the country to the city, but even the London Season was determined by the timing of the hunt. The Season began at the end of the hunting period just before Christmas, bringing the gentry back to their city houses, and the Season ended in August, when it was time to return to the country estates for the hunt. The Season allowed just enough time for the sitting of Parliament. Being a fashionable man, Edwards wore a riding coat. Covering the vest, the coat was double-breasted with large lapels to the waist and cut longtailed at the back. The linen shirt underneath had a stiff neck band. The pants were tights, with tall boots worn over them. Edward's neck was adorned by a cloth square folded into a triangle forming a cravat.

The butler showed the solicitor up to the drawing room and left quietly. After the two men had sat down by the fire, the solicitor laid out a number of documents.

"This is the property contract for your signature, Mr Edwards. Here are the receipts for the Exchequer bills and the India bonds you traded on the Stock Exchange. And these are your new railway shares."

"Yes, they should give me a better return than the two percent the landed gentry expect to get from their estates."

"You are certainly right there, Mr Edwards. Finally, the mining shares here. I must congratulate you. They have risen already. The timing was just right, Mr Edwards."

"Yes, I expected that much."

Edwards had relied on his knowledge of mining and geological assaying. After all, he had made his fortune in mining ventures on the goldfields in Australia. Now he reaped the benefits in comfortable style in London. Edwards' mind flashed back to those heady days at Hill End, the booming gold rush town a few days journey out of Sydney. Hunt was just a paid labourer who never took the risk to stake out his own claim, to work without regular income just on the hunch of making it one day. Quite the opposite of Holtermann. Holtermann supported himself with odd jobs besides mining his claim with a partner. For years they found no gold at all. Edwards had joined them after he had analysed the fields in the neighbourhood and reckoned they had to be close to striking gold. He had had his fights with Holtermann. Yes, at times he had really hated him. But they got rich together, first from the gold, then from the rise of their gold mining shares on the stock market. Holtermann was the main share holder. He became even wealthier then Edwards.

For his London solicitor, Edwards was a lucrative client. The solicitor had taken up business following his apprenticeship in law. He was well connected as a member of Society, even though his elder brother had inherited their father's title and the extensive estate.

The solicitor and Edwards had finalised their formalities and had gone on to more personal matters.

"Don't forget to join us for the grouse hunt at my parents' moor in Scotland in August, Mr Edwards. It's an arduous journey, but London will be quite dead after the end of the Season."

"Yes, thanks again for the invitation. I certainly enjoyed my previous stay with your family, particularly partridge shooting at the estate in the Midlands last September and the pheasant season in October."

"And then we have foxhunting in November. Before we know it, we'll all be back in London for Christmas and a new Season." The solicitor rose slowly as he continued. "I'm glad you'll join us. I know it can be tedious at times and expensive. The tips expected from visitors for the myriad of servants can send a man to the poor house."

They laughed heartily and bade each other farewell.

The butler returned. "Mr Hunt acts in a most impolite manner, Sir. He refuses to leave. Shall I have him thrown out?"

Edwards paced the floor, stopped at the fireplace and stared into the flames. Since he's here in London now, I may not be able to avoid him. Even if he doesn't move in my circles, his impertinence may taint my standing in society. Better I stay in control.

Edwards turned around. "Send the wretched character up. Say I can spare a few minutes."

The butler returned with a short thin man who was clutching some newspapers.

"Mr Edwards, Mr Hunt," the butler announced.

The two men shook hands. "Would you care for some tea?" Edwards asked.

"Yes, Sir, thank you."

The butler nodded and left quietly, making his way down two floors to the kitchen in the basement.

Edwards bade his visitor take a seat. "Hunt, you say? Coming from Australia. I was there too, years ago until 1873, mining gold. That's a long time ago."

Hunt was confused. "Of course, Mr Edwards, we worked together for many years. You employed me as your offsider while I was saving up money to start my own claim." The sparkle in Hunt's eyes dimmed. "But then I invested it all in gold shares. I lost everything. Holtermann ruined me. After he'd sold out, the stocks failed. I was not as lucky as you were, Mr Edwards."

"Ah yes, those exciting days." Edwards' thoughts drifted back again. He couldn't let the notion rest that his fortune was just based on simple luck. "It wasn't pure coincidence. Before my partner Hammond and I joined the Holtermann claim, we had studied the area carefully. We were convinced that the direction of Holtermann's excavations had to change in order to hit a goldbearing reef. That's why we got into arguments with Holtermann. He insisted on going deeper rather than sideways. He pulled rank as major owner and mine manager." Edwards remembered how frustrated and angry he had been, how he had plotted to get his way.

Hunt interrupted his thoughts. "Remember the three of us filling in the shaft together when Holtermann and Beyers were away, working like mad to complete the task on our shift, to block the shaft well above bottom and to tunnel sideways? It was too late for Holtermann to change it when he returned. He was furious as hell, wasn't he?" Hunt laughed.

Edwards smiled and shook his head. "When Holtermann and Beyers refused to continue our horizontal drive we worked it alone for a week. And then we struck one of the richest gold veins ever discovered at Hill End. It made our Star of Hope Mine productive for years. What a bonanza we had started!"

The glow from the fire enhanced the warm sentiment the two men felt until Hunt changed the mood with his comment.

"You hated Holtermann. He was so stubborn. Didn't listen to reason, did he? But then he took all the credit. Later in the payoff when you and I found the world's biggest lump of gold quartz, he sent photographs to the newspapers with him standing next to the five-foot rock of gold. Got that photographer fellow to do the job when you and the other partners said no."

"Yes, he was an intolerable pain in the neck in those days, a hypocrite, really!" Edwards knew how at that time he had wanted to see Holtermann humiliated and had suggested so to Hunt.

"That's why you wanted me to get at him," reasoned Hunt.

"You wanted him destroyed. I was very glad when you paid me the advance. I sure needed the money. And I knew you would honour your promise, so here I am."

Edwards swung around quickly towards Hunt and was about to say something when the butler entered and served the tea. After he had left, Hunt continued.

"Well, Sir, Bernhardt Holtermann is dead. He died on his forty-seventh birthday in his mansion in North Sydney. Now I have come to collect the rest of the promised money, Mr Edwards."

Edwards glared at Hunt and then glanced at the headlines of the newspapers Hunt had spread out on the desk. "What are you saying, man? Are you telling me you killed him? Why would you do that? How would you get away with that? The newspapers here say nothing about murder. No word about foul play."

"No, Sir. In fact, I didn't do it myself. I befriended the cook in his household. She hated the upstart, too. Together we found a way to put him in harm's way. That's what you wanted me to do, wasn't it? 'Make the bastard suffer,' you said."

"The man I was then could have said that in a drunken stupor, years ago. I might have suggested humiliating him, showing the world that he had made some serious enemies, indicating that he didn't deserve his glory, his obscene wealth." Edwards sipped his tea in hazed reflection. "But never did I receive any news of an attack on Bernhardt. Nobody assaulted him, broke his bones. In fact I was glad. I thought you must have forgotten our deal, Hunt. After all, it goes back a decade or more. If I gave you some money back then it must have been a loan. Keep it now."

"But Sir, you promised me more. That's why I'm here. My luck had run out in Australia, and I was homesick for England. But now that I have actually made it back, I might as well receive the well deserved reward from our bargain. You can't shake me off that easily. You wouldn't want your reputation tarnished here in London, would you, Mr Edwards?"

Edwards turned his head quickly towards Hunt. Then he leant back and smiled. "Now, Hunt, be realistic. It would do you no good to set your word against mine. I am now well established and well connected here. But more importantly, I have demonstrated my friendship to Bernhardt Holtermann. When he was here with his celebrated photographic exhibition I met him and his wife, Harriet, on many occasions and I gave a ball in their honour that was the talk of the town that Season. He had become a real gentleman, a devoted promoter of Australia, and an intelligent entrepreneur. Bernhardt, Harriet and I parted as caring friends."

Edwards had thought often of the days the Holtermanns had spent with him in London. He had been impressed by the way Bernhardt had changed into a business man who understood the marketability and profit potential of new products he was taking back for production in Australia. Bernhardt had also explained to him the policies he was pursuing in Parliament in Sydney, supporting free international trade and the expansion of local infrastructure for the benefit of commerce and for the growth in population. Edwards also admired Harriet for the social graces she had developed. Her expert knowledge had helped him to organise their ball and to make it a success. But what he could not banish from his mind were the sweet memories of the Holtermanns' travelling companion, Victoria. Her beauty and charm, her compelling eloquence and wit resonated through his memory. Even though he had not been able to fathom her relationship to Bernhardt, Edwards had secretly entertained the idea of his own serious liaison with Victoria. What had finally prevented him from acting was his desire to marry up the social ladder. At that time Edwards had still been hoping to marry into Society. He was pursuing one or two possible prospects. Even now he still was not sure whether the ladies in question had discouraged him eventually, or whether he had found them too dull. What remained was his envy of Bernhardt for having Victoria in his household.

Edwards interrupted his reminiscing to continue his response to Hunt's allegations. "In fact," he exclaimed, "come to think of it, I was vaguely worried about our old scheme against Holtermann and warned him during his visit to be careful should his path ever cross yours again. I warned him not to get too close to you, nor to trust you since you bore an old grudge against him. By that time I was concerned to keep him safe."

Now Hunt realised something that had puzzled him for years. "That explains a thing or two. Not that I was moving in Holtermann's circles, but when my luck really ran out I wanted to ask him for a job, for old time's sake. His people treated me like I had the plague. I never got near him. Our old mateship counted for nothing." Hunt remembered how he was even refused the favour of collecting the ashes, cinders and refuse from the dust bins of Holtermann Hall. From a big household like that he could have earned good money selling it to brick yards and manure makers, not to speak of the finds he might have made by sifting it carefully for inadvertently discarded valuables and other salable items. "Their hostility really strengthened my resolve to cut Holtermann down. And we did. The cook and I, we did it together. Slow poison. She prepared these special German dishes for him. Soon he developed symptoms of dropsy, stomach ulcers, liver problems. We…"

Edwards raised his hand. "Please, no more. I can't stand it. Didn't I tell you, I admired that man? He was my friend. Whatever you did, it must be criminal. But above all, it's deeply regrettable and unspeakably sad. Such a waste. What an inspired and cosmopolitan mind he had, always growing, always seeking new frontiers. Such a family man, fond father of five children! Such a versatile entrepreneur and businessman. His life had a real purpose, to promote Australia to the world, to educate people and to enrich their minds. Such an artist, winning international prizes for his breakthrough photography. A Member of Parliament with far reaching proposals for the development of his young country."

Edwards' eyes were moist and he could speak no more. Hunt was at his wits end. He gestured and opened his mouth, then stopped before any word came out. Edwards turned to his desk. He stared at the Sydney newspapers and then rang the bell for the butler. "Mr Hunt is leaving," he told the servant.

With his head low between his narrow shoulders, Hunt shuffled out. He did not bother to take the newspapers, nor even his hat.

Edwards remained seated at his desk, filled with remorse and grief, his face buried in his hands. He thought of Bernhardt, hearing him talk with characteristic enthusiasm in his German accent. Edwards had always hoped to meet his friend again, to share a few laughs, to discuss the latest world trends in business and in politics. The chance had passed forever. Suddenly Victoria appeared before Edwards' inner eye in all her grace and beauty. Who would be looking after her in the changes that were now bound to take place in Holtermann's household? Edwards had thought of her often and he cared for her. Re-examining the possibilities regarding Victoria, even if she lived at the other end of the earth, Edwards cheered up.

As Hunt stepped out, the London day had turned raw with a cold rain. The clouds had descended into the city trapping the smoke and mixing it with the fog, creating a dense, yellow, fetid haze. The sky had turned dark with the smoke from thousands of coal fires lit in the morning to warm bedrooms and dining rooms and to cook breakfast. Flakes of soot drifted moistly from all chimney tops. Having left the better part of London, Hunt now walked in muddy streets where piles of horse manure emanated the stink of a stableyard. Some women had pattens strapped under their shoes, metal rings on small stilts that kept them an inch off the ground. A crossing sweeper cleaned a path across the street before a gentleman walked to the other side, paying a penny for the service. Hunt gagged as he caught a drift from the Thames, the river that carried the untreated sewage of the millions of city-dwellers and factories and workshops along the river's banks. Hunt had trouble breathing, his head was pounding. He was vexed by the noise around him, the rattling of wheels and clacking of hooves on the pavement, the click of women's pattens, the bell of the muffin man, the shrill cries of street peddlers, the din of a hurdy-gurdy player. In the streets, carriages almost dashed into each other in ill-tempered manoeuvres. Mud and horse manure were splashed around by churning wheels, by flying hooves, by stamping pedestrians. Hunt walked without an umbrella, catching the runoff from those of other people jostling and sliding around him, water running down his neck, across his face. The day had turned dark, icy, stinking and hostile. Hunt walked on towards his meagre accommodation, shivering, sneezing, wheezing and coughing. He was so wet, nobody could see he was crying. "I am damned," he whimpered. "What am I doing here? This is not the place I remembered during all those years abroad. I recalled my youth in a golden city, my parents, my mates. All gone, grown strange. I'll never earn another passage to Sydney. Why did I have to leave that place where I lived royally on pennies, where the breeze carries the scent of blossoms all year long? Even the rain is warm there. Why did I abandon my fishing dinghy on the beach in Woolloomooloo Bay where crystal clear water sparkles in the sun? I was mad to come here and I will stay mad for being here! I am damned indeed."

1860

THE HAMBURG HOTEL, SYDNEY TOWN

It all started twenty-five years earlier when the young Bernhardt Holtermann worked as a waiter in Sydney in a King Street hotel called The Hamburg. He had been naturally drawn to the place since he was born and raised in Hamburg and had come from there just two years before. Speaking in German to the owner, Herr Müller, helped him get the job. At twenty-two years of age Bernhardt was a good-looking lad of medium height, a bit underweight for want of money and time to eat well. He sported a fashionably trimmed dark beard. Bernhardt had an agile mind, continuously planning and plotting, how to advance his job, what other opportunities there were, how to make the best of the little spare time he had, preparing outings alone or with mates, considering developments in politics and commerce, re-evaluating the steps he had taken in his life so far, and, of course, the girls, who were always at the forefront of his thinking and yearning, those mysterious, elusive creatures.

To improve his English, Bernhardt devoted some of his limited free time to reading. He was fascinated by a book Mr Müller had lent him, entitled *SYDNEY in 1848*. Even though its contents were dated by twelve years, he read the opening page with pride:

> The principal object of this Work is to remove the erroneous and discreditable notions current in England concerning this City, in common with every thing else connected with the Colony. We shall endeavour to represent Sydney as it really is –to exhibit its spacious Gas-lit Streets, crowded by an active and thriving Population –its Public Edifices, and its sump-

tuous Shops, which boldly claim a comparison with those of London itself; and to show that the Colonists have not been inattentive to matters of higher import, we shall display to our Readers the beautiful and commodious Buildings raised by piety and industry for the use of Religion. It is true, all are not yet in a state of completion; but, be it remembered, that what was done gradually in England, in the course of many centuries, has been here effected in the comparatively short period of sixty years. Our object, in setting forth this Work, is one of no mean-moment; and we trust that every Australian, whether this be his native or adopted country, will heartily bid us "God speed!"

In the book Bernhardt studied the copper-plate engravings showing the sequence of buildings of all major streets in vertical perspective as seen by a passer by, rendering each house in architectural detail. He read the comments on major edifices, like The Royal Hotel, describing the division of rooms, entertainment halls and restaurants of the five storey structure and noting their changing uses through the years. Bernhardt also savoured general comments in the book, putting a historical perspective on modern developments:

This has been truly called the age of action, and of quick and rapid events. In our previous chapter we described the state of things in 1790, when, at one period, there was not in the colony four months provisions for the entire population, even on the most reduced scale; and when several persons had perished of inanition before the arrival of the transports from the Cape, bringing part of the stores saved from the Guardian and now, by a stroke of the enchanter's wand, we find the scene rapidly changed, and ourselves introducing our readers to a far different state of things: –our denizens of the pasturage-plains boiling down into tallow sufficient meat to feed nearly half a million of persons, because we have not mouths to eat it; and our denizens of the city luxuriating in all the delicacies which the well appointed hotels and restaurants of Sydney afford on the most princely scale.

Bernhardt had also stumbled onto some different reading material. This related to two sisters who stayed with their chaperone at the Hamburg Hotel. They were just a bit younger than Bernhardt and he had been attracted to them since he had first laid eyes on them. Mr Müller had introduced Bernhardt to the ladies in passing. Mary's hair had a tinge of red, reflecting her Irish descent. Her narrow lips made her appear a bit serious and stern. Bernhardt was taken by the older sister Harriet, by her enchanting smile, her pronounced cheek bones, her classy chin and nose, her sparkling eyes, her full head of dark hair. Even though her whole body was hidden from neck to feet by a chaste dress, Bernhardt could deduce the perfectly shaped body beneath it. Subconsciously Harriet reminded Bernhardt of an old picture of his mother when she was young. Since Harriet and Bernhardt had been introduced, he used every opportunity to chat with the three ladies, inquiring about their comings and goings, their background in general, about Harriet's moods and fancies. She responded to his approaches with queries about Sydneytown and about his life here and abroad. Before Bernhardt fell asleep after a long day's work, he fantasised about getting close to Harriet. When he was woken with a rough call early in the morning he looked forward to the day because he would certainly see Harriet again, would be able to savour her smile, to look deep into her beautiful eyes, and listen to her witty conversation.

One day while the ladies were out, some parcels were delivered for them from a store and Bernhardt was told to take them up to the ladies' rooms. There he saw some papers on the desk. From the letterhead he noticed that they had been written by Harriet, and he stole the time to read a sheet. He couldn't decide whether it was a letter to her parents or to a friend, or a travelogue she was sending to a newspaper, perhaps in her hometown of Bathurst. Whatever it was, Bernhardt was captivated as soon as he started reading:

> The young ladies of Sydney are in many respects remarkable. They have more ribbons, jewels, and admirers, than perhaps any other young ladies of the same age in the universe. They prattle –and very insipidly too –from morning till night. They rush to the Botanical Gardens twice a week, to hear the band play, dressed precisely after the frontispiece in the latest imported number of Le Follet. They wear as much gold chain as the Lord Mayor in his state robes. As they walk you hear the tinkle of their bunches of charms and nuggets, as if they carried bells on their fingers and rings on their toes. The first time I visited the theatre I sat near a young lady who wore at least a half-a-dozen rings over her white gloves, and who, if bare mosquito-bitten shoulders may be deemed beautiful, showed more beauty than I ever saw a young lady display before.

Bernhardt put down the paper where he had found it and smiled. He knew he had to return to work downstairs, but he took another manuscript from the rear of the desk top and started to read it as quickly as he could, which wasn't very fast at all.

> There are two Circuses in town, in each of which pantomimes are performed, as well as astonishing feats of equestrianism. There is also a menagerie in Elizabeth Street, which contains an elephant, two or three monkeys, a lion and lioness, and a few other animals of the cat species. I was told that in summertime, these animals are kept in a wooden building in the street, and on the setting in of the cooler season they are removed to Botany Bay. In Hunter Street there is a museum of

natural history. This place has a shop front, and the window contains beautiful specimens of preserved animals. A fine gazelle is seen standing in a listening attitude, and several specimens of that curious little animal, the duckbilled mole, kangaroos, opossums, bandecoots, and dingoes, and many of the feathered tribe of Australia and the islands of the Pacific. There is another museum close to the college on the Woolloomooloo Road in Darlinghurst. It is free to the public once a week, on Tuesdays. In the garden, there is a large skeleton of a whale. The interior contains specimens of the war-weapons and other rudely manufactured articles of the savage tribes who inhabit the numerous Australasian islands, and shells and other marine curiosities ad infinitum.

Bernhardt left Harriet's room deeply impressed by her power of observation and by her eloquence of expression. To be able to write English like that, he marvelled. What a clear and elegant language. Of course he had himself learned quite a few new trade expressions lately. He was now familiar with the colloquial terms used in the hotel's drinking establishment. A measure of liquor was called a nobbler, and to pay for a drink was to shout, to stand or to sacrifice. Some of the more exotic beverages had names like stonefence, made from gingerbeer and brandy; spider, lemonade and brandy; constitutional, brandy, bitters and sugar; Catherine Hayes claret, sugar and orange; Madame Bishop, port, sugar and nutmeg; or Lola Montez, Old Tom, ginger, lemon and hot water. At the pub they also served simple meals, like bread and cheese, called roll and rind, or salad, for some reason termed Nebuchadnezzar.

Of course, in the tavern of the hotel Bernhardt never caught a glimpse of Harriet. Under the watchful eye of their chaperone, the sisters stayed well away from the pub, which was a favourite haunt of lusty gold diggers when they came to the city. As Bernhardt thought of Harriet while he was washing glasses at the bar, he listened across the smoke-filled room to a young bearded singer who tried to make himself heard with his mandolin and a song over the din of storytelling and raucous laughter.

> *... the clergy may damn us in hell,*
> *we will not worship the god they serve,*
> *the god of greed who feeds the rich*
> *while poor men languish in the diggers' ditch.*
> *We work hard, we together need no swords,*
> *we will not bow to masters or pay rent to lords.*
> *We are free men, though we are poor.*
> *You diggers all stand up ...*

On went the melody in monotonous rhymes as Bernhardt continued to serve in the bar. The evening drew late. Business slowed and Bernhardt found a chance to step into the parlour to talk to Harriet once more.

As she talked to him she walked him to a quiet corner of the room away from her sister and their chaperone. "So you didn't go to Adelong after all," Harriet was smiling. "With that rich goldminer the other day?"

"I just can't tear myself away now that you are here in town, Miss Emmett," he replied in jest. He sat down to give his tired legs a short rest. "But even if I didn't leave now, I don't want to be a waiter for the rest of my life. It's not my type of job. There's not much money in it either, at eight shillings per week. Most patrons don't tip, except for the odd drunk digger wasting his fortune."

"Perhaps one day you can run your own hotel," Harriet suggested.

"Well, if it takes that to win you, I certainly will make it my life's ambition," he laughed. "If only I could find my brother Franz. He came over here before me. We could start a business together."

"Is that why you came to Australia, to meet up with your brother?"

"Not really. It gave me the idea, but the main thing was to avoid being drafted into the German army. Also, my father's merchant business is going to my elder brother. I have to find my own career and I saw no opportunities back home. Anyway, when you are young you need to see what the world is like beyond your own backyard. You crave a bit of adventure abroad." Bernhardt remembered how he had felt stifled by the strict order of life back home, confined by the feeling that he was assigned to a fixed station in society. People's perceptions of him and assumptions about him seemed to define his life. He saw no avenue to follow his own ambitions. "I couldn't go to the German colonies if I wanted to avoid the draft, so some exotic places in Africa or New Guinea were out. I didn't fancy the French colonies in Africa or Indochina, because the French impress me as being arrogant. America I found a bit too wild. So I opted for what I thought to be exotic Australia."

Harriet laughed. "Exotic, what a stretch of the imagination!"

"Yes," Bernhardt smiled and nodded his head. "That's what you expect Australia to be when you live in Europe. I had no idea Sydney was as civilised a place as Hamburg. Not the exotic colonial outpost at all, just a beautiful, worldly city."

Harriet admired his enthusiasm. "You seem to have fallen in love with this town. But aren't you supposed to fall in love with people?"

Bernhardt was surprised and blurted out in German, *"Mit Ihnen, Liebste!"* confirming his desires for her, before he continued with more control, "Rest assured, I have plenty of reserves left for all occasions. I just haven't expressed my adoration for you yet, Miss Emmett!"

"Don't waste your breath, Mr Holtermann," she smiled pensively. "Flattery will get you nowhere. I would never know whether I could trust an adventurer like you, here today, gone tomorrow."

Bernhardt didn't see himself as an adventurer, just a person who wanted to get ahead in life, who tried to take into account all possibilities. He had not left his family and friends in Hamburg lightheartedly. The decision to go abroad and the uncertain expectations overseas had put a strain on him nobody had perceived. Before the departure he had developed agonising stomach pains. He was overwhelmed by the vast distance of the journey that lay before him. Most likely he would never be able to return. First he took a boat to Liverpool where he was frustrated by his lack of English. On the ocean voyage from Liverpool onwards he had time to relax during the endless days on the *Salem*, but not in comfort, given the pitiable conditions. The sundry throng of migrants and sailors spent well over three months together on the crowded ship. After several people had died, either from malnutrition or from sheer melancholy, and with the passengers languishing from boredom, Bernhardt took the initiative. He got the captain's permission to start an exercise program. No more people died from that time on. Bernhardt ended the journey with a sense of achievement and good comradeship. But after arriving in Sydney he was on his own again. He walked the city streets on a Sunday when all the businesses and pubs were closed and the usual bustle was missing. The sun drenched streets were almost empty. A baking wind blew dust and powdered horse dung into his eyes. Bernhardt felt lost and depressed, questioning his decision to have made the journey. The next day his mood changed as he walked from Hyde Park to the Botanic Gardens, right down to the water's edge. The rich exotic trees and shrubs elated him and he found himself humming a tune for joy.

He tried to find work, but was unsuccessful at first. The only job he got eventually was on a ship again, as steward on a Pacific Island trader, a vessel travelling between Sydney and New Caledonia. Finding work was essential. How else would he live? Coming back to Sydney with an improved command of English, he advanced to employment as assistant in a photographic studio. He learned about the modern technology of cameras, lenses, wet plate glass negatives, dark rooms, and chemicals to coat the negatives before exposure and to develop them afterwards. Bernhardt admired the families whose portraits they took, dressed from head to toe in elaborate gowns and suits. The owner of the shop knew how to charm his clientele. Privately he was a gambling man. Convinced he could become rich that way, he lost much more than the shop could afford. Eventually he sent the business bankrupt. Bernhardt had taken a deep interest in photographic technology, but all the equipment had to be sold off when the shop was forced to close. The young immigrant had to look for another job once more.

"I'm not an adventurer," Bernhardt smiled at Harriet, shaking his head. "I just feel I'm responsible for my own life and for what I make of it. I didn't like the circumstances I found myself in back home, so I did something about it. There is so much to discover and to learn. But I believe I can be diligent and persistent. I'll work my way up. I'm flexible, my talents cover many fields." He smiled deviously. "Yes, many fields," he repeated and squeezed her arm.

"Don't try to take advantage of me, young man. Never underestimate us colonial girls from Bathurst. We know what we want and what it takes. I like talking to you, Mr Holtermann, but you have to attain a reasonable position in society first, to be taken really seriously by an eligible lady."

"I know what you mean, Miss Emmett. I've seen how graciously some people live here. In my last job, when I was a groom on the estate in North Sydney, I got a glimpse of that good life. This is the image that shines before my eyes. I won't stop working for that picture, diligently and cleverly."

They were interrupted. Bernhardt was called out to the bar where a patron had spilt his ale.

Bernhardt went over to clean the table with a rag. One guest had beer all over his trousers. *"So ein Dummkopf!"* he complained.

"You speak German," Bernhardt said to him.

"Of course, I am from Posen. That's actually in Poland, but we speak German there. My name is Louis Beyers."

The two men shook hands. "Holtermann, from Hamburg. I got here two years ago. In the meantime I have even learnt to speak English."

"Ausgezeichnet, junger Mann!" Beyers complimented in German. "Then you like it here?"

"I like it well enough. Better than grey, damp Hamburg. Here I can enjoy the sun and the mild climate by the sea."

Bernhardt loved Sydneytown. He knew it had its filthy parts, like the harbour area called The Rocks, where somebody had once emptied a chamber pot from an upper floor window all over him. When he went on walks he preferred the upper town, Macquarie Street and the parks down to Woolloomooloo. He marvelled at the huge trees, green all year –palms, eucalyptus, Norfolk Island pines, Moreton Bay figs. He relished beautiful Jackson Bay in the middle of the city where he would stroll east for a swim at a sandy beach, watching the manoeuvres of fishing boats and dapper sailing vessels. If he was lucky he caught sight of a windjammer majestically sailing in from the ocean between the steep cliffs of the heads. Bernhardt continued, "I like the bustle of the commercial area in Sydney. I am looking for a business to set myself up, but I have no capital," he laughed.

"Bring us another round, mate," a guest called. "My shout." As Bernhardt returned to the table the patrons were talking about spectacular theatrical performances they had seen in Sydney.

"Lola Montez, now there was a star," one guest was raving. "You should have seen her wild 'Spider Dance'! Actually, she became quite famous as an actress in America after she left here."

"Yes," Bernhardt added to the story, "and before she came here she was also well known in Germany, not so much as a performer, but as the mistress of King Ludwig of Bavaria. He spent so much government money on Lola that they put him into the loony bin." They all laughed heartily.

Beyers picked up the conversation with Bernhardt again. "You'll never make enough money in an ordinary job to set up a business. You just make ends meet. Now that you're here, you should go to the goldfields. You might work for nothing as I have done so far, but you never know, you might strike it rich. Or you might make a decent living from it, as our friends Hammond and Edwards here do."

Beyers introduced Holtermann to the three other men at the table. "Yes," Hammond confirmed, turning his head, indicating approval, "there certainly is gold in Hill End. But mining might not suit city folk. The work is heavy and far less pleasant there in the dirt and the rock tunnels than here."

"But it's worth trying," Edwards added. And it doesn't depend just on luck either. Not all claims are equally promising. And you have to judge how far to dig down, where to branch out.

"Lately, people here in Sydney seem to talk about nothing else but the goldfields and the fortunes being made there," Holtermann marvelled. "Actually, I've seen the big lumps of reef gold quartz from Hill End myself in a shop window in Kent Street here," he beamed. "Imagine finding a nugget like that! Anyway, I don't see much of a future for me here. But what if I dig and dig and find nothing? I don't have any savings."

"You can always get some odd jobs," Beyers explained. "I've had to do it. I've helped out in shops, or been paid by the hour on somebody else's claim once in a while. Look at

Hunt here, he works for Edwards all the time, doesn't even have a share in a syndicate."

"No, I wouldn't like that," Holtermann stated. "I might as well stay here if that's the case."

"Come now," Hunt said indignantly, "we can't all be successful claim owners."

"I didn't mean to offend you, but I wouldn't mind being a successful miner, working my own claim. If I go to Hill End I'll go to strike it rich! And I won't stop digging, till I am rich."

"That's the spirit," Hammond applauded. "Talk to Louis some more. I'm sure he can set you up. He knows his way around Hill End."

"It'd be my pleasure," Beyers agreed. "If you like, we can meet again tomorrow and talk about it. You really should give it a try. What can you lose? Who knows, we could strike it rich together, *Landsmann*," he said, referring to their common background.

Holtermann went back to the counter and spoke to the owner of the hotel. "Herr Müller, there is another German over there, quite a nice fellow."

"I see. I'll go over and talk with him. But I have to lock up soon. It's closing time."

"Would it be all right if we play a game of cards in the parlour after we're finished? Perhaps you would care to join us."

"You waiters are incorrigible. And I'm sure you want Mary and Harriet Emmett to be in it too. You know these young ladies are from a family of good standing. You mustn't get too involved with them, Bernhardt."

"Of course not, Sir," Bernhardt smiled deviously. "For good cheer we could play, Pope Joan with a few stakes on your game board. Who knows, you may land on, King, or the girls on, Matrimony, which would give us a few laughs."

"It's a bit silly, that game. I would prefer, Commerce played for half farthings, so nobody can lose much."

"All right, let's try that. I think they call it poker now," Bernhardt nodded his head. "It's just that after a day's work it feels too early to go to bed straight away. I might ask Beyers there to join us, if it's all right with you."

"Yes, do that, and count me in, too."

The singer was finishing with a lyrical ballad ending in the words:

> There is a river in the range I love to think about;
> perhaps the searching feet of change havenever found it out.
> Ah! oftentimes I used to look upon its banks, and long
> to steal the beauty of that brook, and put it in my song.

The last patrons were leaving. Beyers stayed, talking with Müller at the bar, before the three men went across to the parlour, joining Mary, Harriet and their chaperone. Bernhardt had asked the ladies earlier to stay for the card game. Müller introduced Beyers. The group settled down at a round table in the corner. Bernhardt made sure he sat next to Harriet. Louis Beyers sat beside Mary and seemed to get on well with her. The cards were shuffled and first hands were dealt. The fortunes of the game ebbed and flowed. Bernhardt won some wild bluffs until the others caught on and challenged his bids. Louis risked little and won little. The girls were new to the game and needed frequent advice from Bernhardt and Louis.

The lamps burnt low and eyelids grew heavy. A final round was played before the chairs were pushed back. Bernhardt took Harriet aside. "Tomorrow," he said, "it's my day off work, and I am meeting Beyers to talk about going to the goldfields. Would you ladies care to join us later for afternoon tea? I had the impression your sister Mary doesn't mind Mr Beyers' company, and I certainly don't mind yours, Miss Emmett, dear."

"Talking about minding, young man, I'd advise you to

mind your manners!" Harriet smiled and slapped his arm gently. "But afternoon tea with you should be quite safe," she quipped. "It would be a pleasure, Sir." She bowed graciously.

"I trust I'll be able to get our party there. Just let me know the time and place."

Bernhardt held her arm briefly and they looked deep into each other's eyes, forgetting their surroundings, the chatter behind them. Harriet drew away reluctantly. They joined the others. The girls received shy goodnight kisses on the cheek. Last smiles and glances were exchanged and off they went to their rooms.

Harriet tried to control the warm feelings she had for Bernhardt. It was exciting to be with him, but he was simply not of sufficient financial resources to be considered as a prospective husband. Some marriages appeared strange to her. There appeared to be very little shared between husband and wife, with the woman being sidelined to bearing children and running the household. Harriet saw some marriage opportunities for herself, but she wasn't attracted to living with a husband who still preferred his old friends and his business. Some even wanted the occasional liaison thrown in. She expected things would be different with a man like Bernhardt, if only he had the means to be eligible.

Harriet didn't feel like going to bed yet. By the light of the candle she reread another note she had created with ink and feather earlier that day about her observations in Sydney.

> The buses took my instant fancy, especially those with four or even five horses, doubledeckers upon whose top storey I am not allowed to go. For the outside passengers, exclusively males, climb up at the back by a series of spider steps, hand over hand, and then sit back to back with their feet braced against a rail. Our bus travel is mostly on singleseaters and always in the "inside," which is reached by two broad steps. Buses are furnished with two carpet cushioned seats facing

each other along the length of the vehicle, and there is straw on the floor. These interiors are lit at night by a flickering candle behind a little glass door that seldom keeps shut and swings to and fro with the motion of the bus. You pay your fare through an ingenious partition of glass, behind which appears the driver's left hand to give you change. You ring a bell to tell him you are passing your money up, and he rings the bell very vigorously if any dilatory passenger neglects to tender the fare.

Hansom cabs don't impress me so much. They are gloomy looking things of black or dark blue, while the buses are always painted a brilliant yellow. There is not much to see from inside a cab except the horse's tail and hindquarters. The only excitement with cabs I have seen's when they were coming back from the races at Randwick and raced each other along Botany Street, especially if the hirers had backed a winner. Also I observed cabs on Sunday afternoon, with blinds down and the horse trotting decorously, on the way to Coogee or Maroubra bearing a freight of flirtatious couples. This is the nearest to Tail Eight Avenue that Sydney gets, and even then there is always the driver for chaperone, sitting above his little world and with his passengers well under his eye through the spyhole in the roof.

1860

HILL END

"What an endless and desolate country," Bernhardt wheezed as they struggled up another hill, heavy loads on their backs.

Louis didn't reply. Bernhardt tripped and staggered under the weight of his swag. "I see now only one possible ending for this dreary journey. It will end when I drop dead. Who would have thought I would end up this way, at my age, after all the adventures and dangers I have survived already?"

"Dangers?" Louis asked, to fill in time.

"I might not have survived the voyage to Australia on the stinking *Salem*, you know. As we started out, a large piece of timber was dropped on my foot. It crushed my big toe. When you are a steerage passenger nobody worries about you. The infection could have killed me right there. Seasick like a dog, I was ready to die anyway and go into a wet sailor's grave like other passengers. Who would have cared? The cook might have cared, perhaps. I had become friendly with him. He looked after me like a father as I lay sick for two weeks. The captain gave him permission to let me have special rations from the kitchen. All these nice people I will never see again, the cook, the captain, my relatives back in Germany, my brother Franz, wherever he may be in this country, Müller, back in beautiful Sydneytown, and Harriet, dear Miss Emmett, with her charm and humour, fair Harriet."

Louis listened but didn't comment. He was taken with this fellow Holtermann, interested in his stories, and he reckoned the young man would succeed with a little help. "It's not long now," was all he said.

The Blue Mountains were far behind by now. They had crossed the grassy hills around Bathurst, climbed across the pass to the busy little town of Sofala and followed the river from there. Now they were in steep, wooded hills.

Louis continued, "You know, the route through here was only discovered some forty or fifty years ago. Before that, explorers had set out from Sydney along the valleys of the Blue Mountains until they got stopped by the vertical cliffs and had to turn back. Only when they got the idea to follow the ridges they finally found a passage."

"I wish they hadn't!" In the trees a flock of kookaburras broke into a chorus of laughing song, as if they were mocking Bernhardt's words. It made him smile. "You know," he commented, "sometimes I think I am throwing away too much of what I have achieved already. Now I'm starting from scratch again, with no idea of what lies in store for me. Perhaps I should have kept those steady jobs, to work myself up over the years. But how far would I get?" he argued with himself. "Would I be satisfied with that?"

"Yes, how do you know what you can achieve if you don't push to the limit?" Louis agreed. "And how do you know where the limit is?"

"I think I have a few talents," Bernhardt pondered. "I can organise things, take the initiative, and carry through with an idea. And I don't mind rolling up my sleeves and working hard."

"I certainly hope so. That's why I brought you along!"

"But it all has to fit into a larger picture, you know. I have my dreams of what I want to achieve in life, and I can never reach them working for others. I have to be my own man, forging my own fortune. So, I'm on the right track, am I not?"

"Of course you are. Nothing ventured, nothing gained! I understand how you feel, though, out in the wilderness here. It looks like we are going nowhere. But wait 'till we get to Hill End. It's a good town. You'll be surprised. Everything is available in the shops, and there are pubs, too. Imagine that, standing at the bar with an ale in your hand! The people are nice, not as rough and wild as you would expect. They work together and help each other out. You'll find all types, beside the diggers; there are bankers in tailed suits and top hats, merchants in formal wear and bowler hats, and ladies in frilly dresses with white aprons."

"They must be the type of people who pass us in the coach along the road here once in a while," Bernhardt mused. "I really envy them. Even if they get shaken up badly in the coach, it certainly beats walking. But one day we'll be able to afford that, too, Louis!" He slapped his companion's shoulder. "But without my aching feet and without the heavy load on my back I would have enjoyed the scenery around us much more."

Bernhardt had marvelled at the mighty rock walls of the Blue Mountains, at the huge trees standing majestically apart on the slopes. Along the way the wanderers had surprised groups of kangaroos, grazing or resting on their hind legs and their strong tails, tentatively holding up their small front legs, turning their heads curiously at the pair. The men had made out koalas sleeping high up in gum trees. Flocks of white cockatoos had circled overhead, calling down at them with powerful rough cries. Colourful rosellas could be seen playing in the trees. Camping out at night they had seen wombats amble by on their short legs and they had been approached by curious possums which observed the men patiently with big black eyes.

Before reaching Hill End the two men passed the first mining lease. All they saw was a heap of rocks and earth surrounding the top of the vertical mining shaft. Over it, a small ragged roof made of wide pieces of bark, was propped up on thin poles.

"We're almost at the town," Louis exclaimed. He commented on the mine, "See how the roof protects the shaft against the elements, and how the canvas sail is set up below it to deflect the wind into the shaft to provide ventilation?"

"How far does a shaft go down?"

"After a few years of excavating, hundreds of feet."

There was a larger octagonal bark roof nearby, supported by well carpentered struts and braces.

"That's to shelter the horse from sun, rain, and snow while it works the whim for hoisting rock from the shaft."

Bernhardt stopped at the word 'snow', as it hadn't occurred to him that snow would fall in the area. Snow was alien to the Australia he knew. They paused to talk with the two miners working outside, telling them about their journey, and asking them if they'd had any luck in their claim. Yes, they had discovered a thin vein of gold quartz which they hoped would lead them to richer finds. Louis and Bernhardt were eager to finally make it to Hill End. They struggled up one more grassy hill among scattered shrubs and gum trees until they reached a shady spot at the top. There they threw down their bundles. They were overwhelmed to see the town finally spread out below them, hundreds of roofs shimmering in the sun. In the centre stood a massive stone church, its belfry pointing like an index finger into the dark blue sky.

"What a beautiful sight," exclaimed Bernhardt. "It makes me so happy to see it! I thought I wouldn't make it, but now I'm glad I took the challenge. This is the place where we'll make our fortune, Louis."

The men sat in the shade and a gentle breeze cooled their hot, aching limbs.

"You see the two storey brick building?" Louis pointed out. "That's the Australian Joint Stock Bank in Clarke Street. Along the high road you have the apothecary of George Laroche, next to it Kirkpatrick, the mining agent, then the tiny post office. The tall bark building is Jenkins, the blacksmith and shoeing forge, followed by the Arms Hotel. Further on are my friends, Myer and Siefke. They run the tobacconist, bowling saloon and shooting gallery, and then there's the Bank of New South Wales."

"What's the monotonous noise in the background?"

"Ah, the stamper batteries. You'll have to get used to their sound. They run all the time. They crush the gold quartz from all the mines. The quartz rocks get pounded to a powder by steam-driven iron stampers. The gold then is washed out with water and mercury. The gold sticks to the mercury."

"The stamper batteries run day and night?" Bernhardt asked.

"Well, sometimes. We all work day and night. You'll have to get used to that, too," Louis kidded.

"I know, I know, in shifts, right? You take lights down the shaft, candles. It would be dark down there any time of the day."

"You'll be a proper miner yet! You know it'll be hard, dirty work. Often we make only one foot progress during a shift unless we are blasting. But blasting is expensive. We won't have much money." Louis lay on his back, looking up into the tree. "After we get settled at Hill End, let's see if we can acquire a claim together. Should we give it a name, Bernhardt?"

"A name for our claim?" Bernhardt looked at the town below, at the green hills around it, and smiled. "The Star of Hope Mine," he shouted enthusiastically.

"Yes, one day that name will be famous, *mein Freund!*" Louis agreed with the suggestion.

"And we'll be famous with it."

They laughed and hoisted their loads. The descent into town was easy. At the outskirts they saw women in long dark dresses working their vegetable gardens around the houses. Children were playing hide and seek, with much yelling and screaming when anybody was found. The friendly family dog was no help to the children attempting to remain hidden. Some houses had verandas, others were just sitting on the mud. Roofing was made of shingles, or corrugated iron, or huge sections of bark, held down by odd arrangements of saplings and pieces of timber. Bernhardt and Louis heard a group of children singing in school. The men then came to the shops with their large, fancy signs reading J. Kennedy – Practical Tailor, and Meacher & Co –General Warehousement & Wholesale Wine & Spirit Merchants. Manson & Co –Hall of Commerce displayed fine men's clothing and material on the veranda out front. Mrs McDowall's Millinery Emporium boasted an attractive display window. Bernhardt and Louis saw an assortment of huge new barrels at Hudson Bros. & Co, and they admired all the old and new carriages below the large sign of Burgess & Moller's Blacksmithing, Wheelwrighting, Coachbuilding and Farriering Establishment. They passed the Times Printing Office, and greeted a fine looking woman standing in the door of the Colonial Wine & Dining Rooms. Bernhardt was surprised to see the Telegraph Office. After days in the lonely bush he marvelled at the variety of buildings and read most of the business signs. They walked past the white prefabricated timber office of Civil Engineer C. Mayes –Land, Survey, Building & Mining. The street was busy with people and carriages. Louis ran into Fritz Hermann, a tinsmith and introduced him to Bernhardt. Finally, the long journey came to an end at one of the many tobacconists, where Louis rented a room.

On the other side of the world in England a young girl arrived at her exclusive private boarding school for the first time. The girl's name was Victoria. Her mother, a fading beauty, delivered her to the hallowed grounds, trying to hide the influence of a few drinks she had taken to strengthen her for the occasion. At their final farewell the mother broke down into uncontrollable tears, which seemed strange to Victoria, since she felt her mother had always regarded her as a burden. The school was aware of Victoria's simple background, but they accepted her gladly, since all her fees and expenses were guaranteed by a trust in her favour established by an un-named benefactor and administered by a prominent London firm of solicitors.

With the support and encouragement of her teachers, the once shy girl became self-confident and she felt she could make a success of school. She soon had a few good friends who appreciated her wit and her sincerity. When school holidays rolled around and her mother felt indisposed to have her home, Victoria didn't want to be a burden to her wider family who already had enough trouble to make ends meet. She accepted invitations from classmates to spend the time with them at their parents' country estates or at their London townhouses. She was even welcome on their holiday trips. Everybody was glad to assist this deserving, fair and grateful girl.

In her education, Victoria did well in all subjects, but she was particularly fascinated by the geography and history of far away places like South America, California, and Australia. She was amazed that less than a century ago a whole continent like Australia had still been there for the taking and could be claimed by Britain, just as a place to send prisoners. She knew about the overcrowded prison ships permanently moored in London to relieve the land-based prisons, overflowing with thieves and swindlers. Murderers and other serious criminals were hanged anyway, but Victoria recognised that society was polarised so severely between the rich and the poor that crimes of opportunity offered to many a glimpse of hope in their dreary lives.

When America declared its independence from Britain, the swelling number of prisoners could not be transported there any longer. Victoria was surprised that the decision between sending shiploads of prisoners to Africa or to Australia was made on the assumption that Australia had better trees for making ship masts and seemed to offer the opportunity to grow flax to produce linen sails.

Nowadays, of course, transport of prisoners had long stopped, and immigrants went to Australia lured by the prospect of becoming independent and rich with prosperous farms or in burgeoning trades and industry. The latest excitement was created by reports of amazing gold finds on the Australian continent. Wouldn't it be fantastic to see a place like this when she had grown up, the girl marveled, a thriving colony, which she imagined from what she had read, to be quite exotic, yet with civilised and elegant cities like London itself, populated by fancy ladies and handsome, adventurous gentlemen.

1867

THE ALL NATIONS HOTEL

Bernhardt Holtermann never became the typical gold digger. He didn't drink and gamble. He only savoured liquor when a special occasion warranted it. He didn't like the way alcohol muddled his thinking. He preferred to enjoy life with a clear mind. Bernhardt also loathed gambling. He saw it as a futile way in which unfulfilled people tried to prove their worth. What an unproductive waste of time, he thought.

During seven years of back-breaking work, of everyday endless toil down the mine shaft and on additional jobs above, Bernhardt didn't regard mining as his final lot in life. He saw it as a path to move on to his larger aims of becoming a business man and the prosperous head of his future family. Yet, like any other digger, he kept up his drive day by day, year after year, with the hope gleaned from gold finds in other claims throughout the area. For the first few years Bernhardt still felt homesick, which he couldn't quite understand, since he was glad to have come to Australia. He also felt an unending yearning for Harriet, which he found difficult to express in his letters to her. The highlights of his life were the visits to Harriet and her family in Bathurst. Louis Beyers was his companion at work as well as on those rare trips. After seven years, the tireless labour of the two partners in the Star of Hope Mine paid off. They hit a gold bearing vein. The quartz was crushed at the stamper battery, the gold was sold to the bank. Bernhardt and Louis each received a respectable sum of money.

Bernhardt stood in the doorway of his new Hill End hotel in top hat, dark vest, coat and tie, white shirt, and light trousers. He looked out over the front veranda marked by seven timber posts. These supported a fine shingle roof and two signs, one saying, All Nations Hotel, the other, Nonpareil and, All Meals. Bernhardt paused for a moment to savour the mood on this special day. After many desperate years at Hill End he had finally made it. The seemingly endless struggle for survival was over. They had finally struck gold a few months earlier. The vein had run out again, but it had given the partners financial independence and respectability. Bernhardt had built the hotel. Today was one of the greatest days in his life, not only the official opening of the hotel, but also in his private affairs. Bernhardt had never wavered in his desire to marry Harriet Emmett. He had stayed in touch despite the many miles between them. Today he would finally be able to ask for her hand.

The Chinese shopkeeper from across the street walked over to talk with Bernhardt. Chan had watched Bernhardt's rise to budding entrepreneur from when he had worked to support his mining as an occasional assistant in Chan's shop. Bernhardt made it a point to be friendly with people who were not of British origin, since he himself wasn't British and he felt derided at times by the official colonists.

"Congratulations on the opening of your hotel, Esquire," Chan exclaimed. "A fine addition to Clarke Street and to Hill End. You are moving up in the world."

"You are right, Chan. Yes, money needs to be invested and put to work."

Bernhardt remembered the business alternatives he had considered after the gold strike. First he had thought of setting up a photographic shop, putting to work his experience from the studio in Sydney. He could have photographed all business establishments at Hill End and in nearby towns for a fee, recording and publicising the progress being made in Australia, depicting the world being created. But to operate a proper shop he would have needed an experienced partner. To run the hotel he needed less skilled help. It seemed to make better business sense. It would give him the security he could not rely on in mining.

Bernhardt turned to Chan and heard him say, "Well, you know me, I'm not into mining at all. I just keep all you hard working men well supplied with wholesome produce, so you can keep up your strength."

"Yes, you are a good businessman, and a good friend. Come on in and have a drink on the house with me and Franz. Did I tell you that I finally found my brother Franz at a settlement not far from here, up the Macquarie River, a place with the strangest name, Root Hog or Die." They laughed heartily.

"Well, let's go in and celebrate, Chan."

At the bar Chan and Franz toasted each other.

"I'll let you in on a secret," Bernhardt told them. "This is a fateful day in more than one way. We'll have a bit of an opening celebration for the hotel and I've invited Edward Emmett of Bathurst and his family to join us. That's Harriet and Mary's father. He agreed to come down. Harriet and I met at the Hamburg Hotel in Sydney in 1860. We got on pretty well right from the start. Louis met Mary there on a visit, when I introduced them. We kept in touch with the two sisters all these years. Fond letters back and forth, you know the way it is. Well, we went to Bathurst as often as we could get away, but certainly not often enough. The Emmetts are really nice people."

"Now you are all set," Franz grinned, "with money in the bank."

"Yes, that's why I spoke to Mr Emmett the last time I visited them, and he had no serious objection. Today Louis and I will make it official, we'll both ask for their hands in marriage." Bernhardt beamed in anticipation.

"Absolutely wonderful," exclaimed Chan. "I wish you luck today and for your marriage!

"*Du hast meinen Segen, Bruder,*" Franz gave his blessing and slapped his brother's back.

Bernhardt went around to greet the first guests. He felt gratified and excited but at the same time uneasy about being the focus of the event. Mark Hammond came in, followed by Edwards and Hunt, and by William Slack, another hotel keeper from further down the road. Bernhardt went to greet him.

"Bill, great to see you. Thanks for coming over."

"Well, I had to wish you success, not too much success, of course. We needed another hotel here in town. Hill End is growing so quickly. Congratulations. You're doing well for your age. Are you giving up mining then?"

"Giving up mining? Bill, how could I? There's still plenty of gold out there. I wouldn't want to miss my share of it. We'll certainly drive our shaft deeper."

"You'll be a very busy man. The hotel alone keeps me running day and night. Family has to be there all the time, otherwise you don't know where the money goes, but you do have your brother here to help you. That's good."

"Yes, family. If you stick around long enough today you might hear some more about that. I have my plans." Bernhardt smiled and left him guessing.

Louis arrived wearing a new outfit, all signs of miner's dust well scrubbed away. The Emmetts' carriage rolled up and Bernhardt and Louis welcomed the parents respectfully. The girls were greeted with restrained hugs and kisses, as the young couples could scarcely control their excitement in front of the parents.

The family was treated to a drawn out luncheon, with considerable gaps between courses, as the kitchen help was inexperienced. During the long meal Bernhardt and Harriet had occasion to gaze into each other's eyes. Louis did his best to restrain Mary's bouts of giggling. After the meal, with the excuse of showing her around, Bernhardt took Harriet for a walk. He could not wait to put his arm around her to feel her tender body. They told each other what they had been doing since they had last seen each other. Between teasing and necking Bernhardt also introduced more serious considerations, mentioning how he had talked to Mr Emmett about financial aspects during the last visit to Bathurst. Bernhardt had given some details on how he was now positioned to support a family and Mr Emmett had explained what dowry Harriet would bring into a marriage. Bernhardt reminded Harriet of the first days after they had met in Sydney. All those years earlier she had put the idea into his head to own a hotel one day. Ever since, she had been his dream and his inspiration. There had been no happier times then when he had been able to visit her in Bathurst, he explained. Bernhardt put his arm around Harriet's shoulders and told her he intended to ask her father for her hand in marriage that day. Harriet was radiant, even though she had hoped for and expected this as his purpose behind today's family invitation. The two held each other, and before returning to the inn they ducked into a laneway to steal some passionate kisses.

On their return, Mark Hammond climbed onto the musician's platform in the corner. Nervously he pulled his coat straight, cleared his voice and waved his arms to attract the attention of the people who now filled the room. Somebody whistled energetically and the chatter abated.

"I would like to propose a toast to our new innkeeper, Bernhardt Holtermann, so make sure you don't have an empty glass, which is an unpleasant condition anyway." The laughter of the assembled guests relaxed the speaker a bit, but he kept his hands firmly clasped for security. "I would like to congratulate Bernhardt on his accomplishment in erecting and opening this establishment and I want to wish him every success for the future."

"Hear, hear," came the affirmations, "Good on you."

"I have known our new innkeeper for as long as any of you here, except for the lovely sisters Emmett who honour us with their presence today in the company of their respected parents. In seven years I've had time to observe Bernhardt here at Hill End. There would be few who have worked their claim harder. He has not been as lucky as some of us, but that has never weakened his resolve. Often the gold he extracted with his partner was not enough to pay the Government Gold Commissioner the onerous licence fee for the claim, let alone to sustain a living. As he tried to make ends meet and keep the mine going, we all were able to watch Bernhardt's tenacity and talents in many areas. He took any job that would earn him a few pennies, whether it was at Chan's shop, or as a butcher, or as a baker, or even practicing to be a hotelier, as rumour has it, in running a sly grog shop."

"We wouldn't know about that," came some comments among the snickering.

"The most imaginative way to make money must have been Bernhardt's alternate use of the huge baker's mixing trough. Since baking starts early in the morning, the trough wasn't used during the day. So, when the Macquarie River was too high to ford, Bernhardt took the long baker's trough down to the water and used it to ferry paying passengers across the river. He wasn't worried about making a fool of himself. He knew what he wanted, and now it has paid off. After endless years of hard work the, Star of Hope Mine has finally lived up to its name. Even though this first reef has waned, I am sure there is more gold to come. But now, Bernhardt doesn't depend on those fickle fortunes alone. While still a young man he is now the proud owner and manager of the brand new All Nations Hotel. I am certain he will make a success of his venture. With his convivial and openminded nature, he will not be short of our patronage.

"Hear, hear," came the calls. "Any excuse is good enough!"

"It is in this spirit that I would like to ask you to raise your glasses and to drink a toast to our new innkeeper, Bernhardt Holtermann."

"To Bernhardt Holtermann," the crowd repeated and a few guests started singing, "For he's a jolly good fellow," joined by the whole gathering, "For he's a jolly good fellow," and raising their voices to an uneven crescendo, "For he's a jolly good fellow and so say all of us."

Prompted by, "Hip, hip, hurrah," the tune was repeated.

Bernhardt went over to Mark, shook his hand and thanked him for his kind words. Then he went back to the table to continue entertaining the Emmett family, as they sat with Louis. Bernhardt sat down beside Mr Emmett and steered the conversation around to more profound matters.

"I feel it is important to find the right balance in life," he explained to Mr Emmett. "This gets sometimes forgotten here with the concentration on work, gold and wealth. With the bit of spare time I have left, I get books from the little library here, now that I can read English. For the first time in my life I can experience the incredible works of Shakespeare and Dickens. What a pleasure it is to read such magical words."

He lent back in reverie, taking a sip from his glass.

"And you bought that book on photography," Harriet said, "when you were last in Bathurst."

"Yes, photography, a truly practical art and science. I hope some day I will have more time to experiment with it, to expand its potential."

"You seem to be involved in lots of things here," Mr Emmett replied. "You have good friends, you help them out and they help you. It's the same with me. We belong to a few clubs and societies in Bathurst. This way we can work for the wider community."

"Yes, we need to do that," Bernhardt agreed, "but to lead really sensible lives we also need a family of our own. Of all my relatives, I only have my brother here now, but he said he wants to move on again. I am almost thirty years old and I think it is time I start my own household. I love Australia and I would really like to become part of it by raising my own family here. Now I have the means to support a wife and children."

Mr Emmett nodded. Harriet's eyes glowed in anticipation. Mrs Emmett turned her head to ensure she wouldn't miss a word. Mary giggled at Louis.

"Mr Emmett," Bernhardt continued, "I have known Harriet for seven years now and we have grown very fond of each other. In fact, we feel we cannot live without each other. Since I have now attained a status that allows me to maintain a family in a respectable way, I would like to ask you for your daughter's hand in marriage."

Mr Emmett nodded again. "I agree with your evaluation of the circumstances, Mr Holtermann. When would the wedding be?"

"You mean you approve?"

"Yes, Bernhardt."

Thrilled at the reply, Bernhardt blurted out, "Next month?"

"Oh, we need more time than that to prepare," Mrs Emmett interjected.

"Soon it'll be Christmas and the summer holiday season in January," Mr Emmett calculated. "Would February be agreeable to you?"

"Yes," Bernhardt approved as he smiled at Harriet.

"You have my blessing, son."

Bernhardt reached over and squeezed Harriet's hand. Mrs Emmett took Mr Emmett's hand. Louis grabbed Mary's hand and raised his voice.

"Mr and Mrs Emmett," he uttered, "I agree with everything that has been said here about work, friendship, and family. I have known your daughter Mary for almost as long as Bernhardt has known Harriet. The four of us have been close friends through all these years while we dug for our luck in the fields out here. Mary and I hold each other in high esteem and my financial circumstances are solid now. I would therefore ask you for Mary's hand in marriage."

"I almost expected that much," Mr Emmett commented cheerfully, "and you, too, have my blessing, Louis."

The two young couples drew close together and spoke softly to each other.

"A double wedding," Mrs Emmett beamed with moist eyes. "You must come to Bathurst. We'll have it at the Church of All Saints. Most of our friends and family are close by. I'll arrange it all by February. There'll be so much to do! We'll have a fine celebration. A double wedding, Harriet, Mary, who would have thought that? Are you happy?"

Mary giggled. As Harriet turned to her mother, Bernhardt's thoughts wandered back to the Hamburg Hotel in Sydney. In his mind's eye he saw the young lady standing in the parlour in her straight, self-assured posture, with her big eyes, her smooth soft skin, her graceful figure, responding with her witty commentary to his boisterous remarks. She was a true daughter of this exciting country. Now she would be his and he would be part of her life. How lucky he was! It had really been worth it to work so doggedly, not to give a damn about what others might have been thinking or saying about him. Life was simply marvelous.

Mr Emmett proposed a toast to the wedding. They all raised their glasses. "To our wedding," they cheered.

Bernhardt leapt onto the small platform where Hammond had stood a while before. The room quietened down.

"Unaccustomed as I am to giving speeches," he began, "I would like to say just a few words, but important words. Firstly, I want to thank my friend Mark for his generous remarks. Second, I would like to make an announcement on behalf of myself and of my partner Louis Beyers. Hear this:

We are both engaged to be married, Louis to Miss Mary Emmett and myself to Harriet Emmett. We'll have a double wedding in Bathurst in February next."

Cheers rang from the crowd as Bernhardt continued. "We are happy to have the Emmett family with us today, and those of you who have not met the sisters Miss Mary and Miss Harriet Emmett earlier, have now an opportunity to convince themselves how lucky Louis and I are. This is an exceedingly happy occasion for me. You know we miners are no great romantics, but I have been dreaming about this day for many years." Bernhardt waved his arm in a concluding gesture. "Thank you to all of you for sharing this important occasion with us."

Followed by cheering and applause, Bernhardt left the platform and returned to Harriet's side where he was greeted with a generous kiss on the cheek, accompanied by further cheers from the guests.

Bernhardt felt hot and excited as he pressed against Harriet's side. He also had a sweeping feeling of satisfaction and gratitude for having been accepted by a well established Australian family and for becoming more part of this unrestrained and beautiful country. Bernhardt's anticipation had come true. Here he could create his own dreams and pursue them, without much hindrance from old social structures, from encrusted ways of thinking, or from overbearing governments. Here people were responsible for their own lives, he thought. We need not blame God or government if we are in trouble, and we need not ask for their blessings either. Bernhardt savoured the setting, the noisy tavern filled with friends and colleagues, the congenial family table he shared. As he looked into Harriet's eyes he felt warm lust rising in his body. Soon they would be together, he thought as he stroked her gentle neck.

1868

AT THE FAMILY HOME

A year later Bernhardt and Harriet were living in their own small house at Hill End, complete with a front fence, a massive stone chimney to one side, and a corrugated iron roof sloping down to the front veranda. Bernhardt awoke at dawn, long before it was time to get up. He didn't move so as not to wake Harriet at his side. What could have been a prosperous and comfortable setting for the young couple had turned into a financial nightmare. His business worries kept Bernhardt awake at this early hour. To fight his distress, he let his mind drift back to the time in Hamburg, when, as a boy, he had first discovered that special feeling the thought of gold released in him, a sentiment of joy and wholesome fulfillment emanating from his stomach and rising to his chest. As a youngster he had read stories of alchemists who had produced gold from lead in medieval times. In his youthful fervour Bernhardt had tried it, too. Secretly he got scrap lead and applied various acids and salts he had obtained from his uncle's warehouse to it. It didn't work. Only the joy of thinking of gold remained. Bernhardt didn't believe this feeling had spurred his desire to come to Australia or on to Hill End. And he didn't think it had led to the decision to sell the All Nations Hotel and to invest all the money in two promising new gold claims in nearby Chambers Creek and Root Hog. He and Harriet had been in a very optimistic frame of mind in their new marriage. They felt they couldn't lose and were convinced the new claims would be more profitable than the hotel. But the two mines had proven hopeless. This week the syndicate had decided to close the operation down. All investment was lost. Bernhardt had no money left. The Star of

Hope Mine was not yielding any gold. And now Harriet was pregnant. Bernhardt felt he had let her down. He was not concerned about himself. He had always survived one way or another and he felt he always would. But that was no longer good enough.

At lunch time that day, the couple sat at the table eating a thin soup and plain, dark bread.

"Well, we were both agreed," Harriet said, shaking her head. "We did think it was a good idea to sell the hotel. We thought it was a safe bet to use the money to participate in these new mines."

Harriet and Bernhardt had had a hard time running the hotel after Franz had left. Then Harriet became pregnant and they realised that she would soon not be able to spend all her time in the hotel either. Bernhardt was still mining as well as managing the hotel. But ultimately, they had bigger plans than just running a hotel.

"Yes, the hotel was too much work for me to run on the side," Bernhardt nodded. "It's more than a fulltime job. Bill Slack had warned me. Busy until late into the night and too little rest."

"It was a bold move, investing all our money in the two new mines." Looking around the room, Harriet thought of the larger picture. "I still think it was right, even if it didn't work out this time. If you don't risk much, you can't gain much, Bernie."

"You are right," Bernhardt agreed, putting his hand on Harriet's arm. "If I wasn't holding out for a big success I wouldn't have stuck it out in the dirt and drudge for so many years." He scraped the bottom of his bowl. "The problem is now that our mine is becoming more expensive to work since it needs timbering. I'm sure there's more gold if we dig deep enough. But progress is so slow. Louis wants us to start using explosives to speed things up. The question is, should we spend our last pennies on food or on blasting powder? You're pregnant and need good nourishment."

Harriet distributed the rest of the soup. "I'll be right. What you need is more partners to share the expenses," she suggested.

"That'll reduce our share of the returns when they start flowing. But you're right. We have no choice, we have to create a larger syndicate. Quite a few people are interested, Klein, Bell, Edwards, and Brown. Even Hammond mentioned once that he might be willing to join us."

"If you start blasting now they'll see how committed you are. That should convince them. Once they're in, further timbering and blasting will be cheaper for us. Use the money, Bernie. I'll talk to Chan. He is a good friend. He'll give us a few staples on credit, so we won't go hungry."

"Yes, we both should keep up our strength, you for the baby and me for digging." He got himself a glass of water. "I'm sorry things have worked out so badly these last few months. If our luck doesn't change, I can always do some more odd jobs around town. But I would prefer to spend more time mining, and to have a few hours left over for you, my dear. I am looking forward to snuggling up with you tonight. But now I must be off. I'll buy a few pounds of blasting powder on my way to the mine."

Harriet took up the coat she was stitching. Bernhardt bent down and kissed her.

"Be careful, extra careful," she said as he went for the door.

"Of course. See you later, my dear."

"Love and kisses, Bernie."

Harriet finished sewing the coat and pressed it with the iron filled with hot charcoal. After ironing some other garments she went outside to water the vegetable garden, which now proved to be an important supplement to their limited provisions.

The afternoon went by with other chores around the house.

At the end of that mild and sunny day Harriet wasn't expecting any bad news when she saw Hunt hurrying towards her, gesticulating as he came closer. Out of breath, he stepped through the garden gate, mumbling partly to Harriet, partly to himself.

"Terrible," he said, shaking his hand. "Absolutely gruesome. I hate this mining. It's not worth it. And you, of all nice people, you deserve better. You shouldn't be here."

"What is it? What's happened?"

"The explosion –Bernhardt."

"What happened to him? Is he hurt?"

"It's bad. Prepare yourself. We took him for dead when we pulled him out of the shaft. His eyes were wide open and rolled back. All you could see were two white balls in a blackened face. He wasn't breathing. Beyers shook him, yelling, 'Don't you die on me!' He shook him hard. Then Bernhardt made a beastly sound. He couldn't get any air, couldn't breathe. Then he forced a few gasps of air. His eyes rolled forward. He looked at us briefly, then he fell unconscious again. But he continued breathing."

"I don't believe it, Hunt. Where is he? Take me to him. On the way tell me how this happened."

They rushed off and Hunt resumed his report. "Louis and Bernhardt prepared a blasting. Bernhardt placed the powder at the bottom of the shaft and lit the fuse. Louis cranked him up with the winch. Then we waited and waited. The powder didn't go off. We all thought the fuse had gone out, so Bernhardt went below to light it again. The winch line was down a hundred and ten feet, just twenty feet from the bottom, when the explosion went off."

"What a stupid thing to do! Why him, why now? Is he still at the mine?"

"No, they rushed him to the hospital tent. He was still unconscious."

"Bernie, my poor Bernie! Let's hurry, Hunt."

"Yes, but prepare yourself for the worst. And expect a horrible sight. He looks all twisted and burnt."

When Harriet saw Bernhardt lying there, broken and motionless, delirium occasionally animating his mangled face at times, it suddenly struck her how silly she had been lately to think their circumstances couldn't get any worse. Things can always get worse, unless you're dead. Maybe death would be better for Bernhardt, though, considering his hopeless condition and the suffering that now lay in store for him. Harriet grasped Bernhardt's hand, feeling its feverish warmth. But she wasn't going to be beaten. She knew her husband, his optimism and his irreverent determination. He was alive and breathing now, and that's all he needed to pull through!

As weeks passed with little visible change, colleagues and friends came to visit, shaking their heads at the sight of the patient. Harriet, carrying their unborn baby, was grieving for Bernhardt, but she managed to hold on to her slim hope for his recovery.

Early one evening, the kitchen table in Holtermann's house served as office for the Star of Hope Mine. Louis had brought a few men to the house who wanted to talk things over with Mrs Holtermann.

Louis explained the situation to Harriet. "We want to see whether we can help you, Harriet, to find out what your plans are. This awful blast that injured Bernhardt so badly actually revealed a bit of gold. We'll have enough now to cover expenses, timber, blasting powder, and so on, but not enough to warrant any payouts to the partners."

"Yes, I understand," nodded Harriet. "And that's why I have no money to pay a miner on wages to do Bernhardt's work. We have no other funds left after losing our investments at Chambers Creek and Root Hog."

"We have a solution that would give you money to live on, and would relieve you of the obligation to pay a miner.

Moses Bell here is willing to pay you one thousand pounds for Bernhardt's share."

It was quiet around the kitchen table. Harriet's head was bent in thought. "No," she said finally, "I can't do that. Bernie would never forgive me when he comes back. He worked that mine for so many years. After all this sacrifice, and in the state he's in now, if he heard he had lost his stake, he would probably give up the fight for life and die."

"With all due respect, Mrs Holtermann," argued Bell, "it's not certain whether he will live. The doctor sees a less than even chance, in which case you would have to sell sooner or later anyway. A thousand pounds is a lot of money. You and your baby could live on that for many years."

"Yes, I can see that. But the baby has not been born yet and Bernie is alive and breathing. As far as I'm concerned, I will see him walking out of that hospital tent on his own two legs. I won't betray him. Let's find another solution." She turned to Louis. "Bernie had mentioned to me before the accident that you had talked about expanding the syndicate." She looked at the men. "I assume you are all interested, now that the mine is yielding gold once more."

"Yes," confirmed Klein. "I don't have a thousand pounds, but I would take a smaller share for a few hundred."

"Same here," nodded Edwards.

"Isn't that what we should do, Louis?" Harriet asked, looking at her brother-in-law. "Enlarge the syndicate. Bernie's work share gets reduced and will be less expensive to pay for. You and I, we both get a dab of money. And you'll gain a bit of extra time to spend with Mary and your new baby."

"I wouldn't mind giving up a fraction of my share as long as I remain a majority partner," Louis commented.

"Of course, same here," Harriet nodded. "I would still want to retain a major stake for Bernie. When we hit that rich reef, he deserves a prize share of it." Harriet smiled optimistically. "And I'd like to ask you for another agreement before I give my consent," Harriet nodded to the men. "When Bernhardt returns to work he'll be Mine Manager."

"Understood," agreed the men.

"Thank you all for your consideration and support," Harriet smiled.

"All right, men," Beyers confirmed, "you can buy your minority shares with work obligations matching your contributions and with equivalent pay outs."

They all expressed their satisfaction.

"Let's all go to the mining office tomorrow and put the deal in writing," Louis concluded. "Don't forget to bring your money. And tomorrow night, Harriet, come over to our place for tea. We have to celebrate at least a little bit under these sad circumstances. And we'll raise a glass to Bernie's recovery."

1869

THE HOSPITAL TENT

After weeks hovering between life and death, Bernhardt suddenly showed signs of improvement. The feverish delirium abated. He recognised Harriet again and was able to talk to her. He asked her to bring the little bottle of 'Life Preserving Drops' from home which he took in addition to prescribed medication. The drops were made from the roots of echinacea flowers and from other herbal extracts. Bernhardt was convinced they would improve his strength and speed his healing. Harriet attended to her duties with the mine and the house. It was hard for her being alone although she had Mary nearby, but Mary was busy with her baby.

Then another disaster. Harriet lost her baby. All the strain, the uncertainty and the meagre nourishment had taken their toll on Harriet's constitution. But she didn't really know the cause of the miscarriage. Afterwards, she was weak and she couldn't fight the onslaught of depression, hating their dreary house in that dirty, noisy, godforsaken town. It was winter; days were short. After sunset, a few steps away from the fire, it was cold and damp. The nights seemed endless with brooding and despair. But then Harriet asked herself what the alternatives might have been in her life. She had not wanted to stay with her parents forever, after she had passed up several earlier marriage opportunities. Apart from Bernhardt's, the only other marriage proposal she had received in the previous year was from an old banker more than twice her age. She had rejected it out of hand. Yes, she had certainly taken the right path, no matter where it would lead her. The important thing now was to stay busy. There was plenty to do in and around the house. She helped her sister Mary with her family and she helped out at the hospital tent. When she visited Bernhardt, Harriet acted cheerfully to keep his spirits up. She soon discovered that putting on a smile for Bernhardt improved her own feelings as well.

As summer approached, Bernhardt began forcing himself to leave his bed, no matter how much it hurt. He couldn't lift himself up if he was lying on his back. The pain was overwhelming. Slowly he'd roll onto his side and push himself into a sitting position with his elbow, letting his legs drop over the side of the bed. Initially his eyes would lose their focus, as painful cramps ran through his back muscles. Gingerly he would reach for the crutches and push himself up. Even standing still or taking a few steps would bring him out in a lather of perspiration. Moaning and exhausted he would lower himself into bed again. A few hours later he would try once more. After several weeks he could take some painful steps around the room, hanging in his crutches, trembling and perspiring.

Despite the pain, Bernhardt had found that old feeling again, warming his chest when he thought of gold. And eventually he felt the same emotion for other thoughts and developing future plans.

The day finally came when he was ready to be discharged to continue recuperation at home. The chaplain stopped by his bed after he had visited some other patients.

"I hear you are going home today," the chaplain smiled and nodded his head in admiration. "Good on you."

"You see, I didn't need your last blessing after all," Bernhardt teased him. "Not yet. I never accepted that I would die and that's why I refused the blessing. Anyway, I am not religious, as I told you. I believe in the everlasting order of the universe, and in a dignified kinship of men down here."

"Me, too," agreed the priest, "among other things. But I'm

not here to convert you," he grinned. "You seem to have plenty of drive and vision to keep you going."

"Yes, I've had enough time here to think about things. That helped me to see a purpose in my life. Not just the family and the lust for gold. Of course, I would be happy to have a large family. But lately I have been dreaming about a wider field. As soon as I am well enough I'll stand for Parliament. I have good friends to back me as a candidate for the New Goldfields Western Division here. When I get into Parliament I can work in support of the miners and of the business people out here."

"What a good idea. You have experience on your side, and you're well known and respected. That should keep you busy, if you also plan to take up your work in the mine again."

"It will still be a while before I can move the old bones well enough for that, but I have to go back. From what I hear there is more and more gold being found in the fields here at Hill End and Tambaroora."

"Yes, our area is turning into the most promising goldfield in Australia. More mines get listed on the stock exchange in Sydney. Reports of rich quartz crushings feed the speculation frenzy in the city."

"It's not just the craving for gold that drives me back, the lure of riches, of an elegant lifestyle. I need money to be able to pursue another goal I have been dreaming about. I want to use my photography to promote Australia around the world. Australia is the most wonderful country, with well developed cities, and beautiful natural features. Along the coast, flora and fauna are just like paradise in this ideal climate. But who in the world knows about it? We need immigrants to fill the vacant spaces, to develop farming and industry, the trades, even the arts. That's why I want gold and money, to be able to champion our country around the world."

"You remind me of a missionary," the chaplain smiled.

"That's what kept me going when I lingered between life

and death. I had these visions of great things I want to do. I couldn't let go. I saw the mansion I was going to build in North Sydney, where I had once worked grooming the horses. I saw Harriet there, our children, servants, friends, parliamentary colleagues. But I didn't stop there. I saw huge photographs being admired by thousands at exhibitions in the great cities of the world. And lately I had one more hope. My health drops. They are a real miracle drug. I think they are assisting my recovery tremendously. I could help thousands of people with them if I had funds to promote their benefits and organise their distribution."

"Stop. This is more than you can do in a lifetime. I see now why you are eager to get going. You've no time to waste. I admire you for it. You have my blessing. And give a bit to the poor and downtrodden along the way when you are rich. You know how it feels to be in the other camp."

"Yes. That's exactly what I am now, poor and downtrodden, but I'm not going to stay here. I'll push myself and I'll get on with it. It'll hurt for a while, but there are larger things to look forward to."

Harriet came in, greeted the chaplain, and kissed Bernhardt.

"How long I have waited for this day, to take you home," she sighed.

"Can I help you, Mr Holtermann?" the chaplain offered.

"No, thanks, I'll walk slowly with my crutches, but I'll walk it, however long it will take. There are just a few things to carry and Harriet can take those."

"All right. I'm off then. It was nice to talk with you. I don't have a conversation like that every day. Go back into the world with all my best wishes, Mr Holtermann. G'day Mrs Holtermann."

With Harriet's help Bernhardt got dressed. He looked pale, frail and bent. Slowly they started on their way home. Harriet was pleased it was a sunny, mild day. Nevertheless, Bernhardt was perspiring. He paused to gather his strength. Smiling at Harriet he shook his head slowly in a mixture of sorrow and admiration. "How hard it must have been for you, my dear, to lose the baby while I was in hospital. You at home all by yourself. What a nightmare. You're so strong. Please accept my thanks for all your endurance, and for your love. From here on, things will look up, I promise you!"

1871

GOLDFIELDS SPECULATORS

Two more years had passed at the booming town of Hill End. After a long recuperation Bernhardt had regained his health and strength. Harriet had finally given birth to a son, but he had died soon after. They were heartbroken, but together they kept going. Finally they had a healthy daughter, Franzesca Sophia. Bernhardt was back working the Star of Hope. In the neighbourhood, more gold laden reefs had been found. The Sydney stock exchange was gripped by gold fever. Shares of new mines proliferated while at the Star of Hope gold output remained negligible.

As planned, Bernhardt Holtermann stood for Parliament. The street posters read, 'November 26th, 1871 Polling Day'. On the eve of the elections, copies of the *Sydney Morning Herald* arrived in the goldfields, containing a letter to the editor written by B. O. Holtermann of Hill End. It commented on unreliable and incorrect reports in newspapers about the goldfields and on the apparent gullibility of investors. Bernhardt didn't mention his own losses, but he had learned the hard way from his investments in the mines at Chambers Creek and Root Hog how quickly such schemes could collapse. The letter warned buyers of newly issued gold shares and told investors to buy only if they were certain of the reliability of the vendors and of the authenticity of the mining leases and claims offered.

'If not, they should better spend a few pounds and look for themselves,' the letter said. The writer continued, 'A man need only go and take up a lease, never mind where, misrepresent the same, and he can raise plenty of money. But for how long? Not for many months, because the paying parties will get tired, give up their interests, and run the whole place down. Several claims are really rich, but no one can tell where the gold is to be found. The oldest digger knows no more than a new chum where the gold is in the ground.'

The next morning Louis arrived at the Holtermanns' home in a hurry.

"The town is going crazy," he told Bernhardt and Harriet nervously. "I just went to vote. People were swearing at me because I am your partner. They are quoting from the article you wrote in the Sydney newspaper. These new investment promoters see their shady business and their easy money threatened."

"Well, good," replied Bernhardt. "That's exactly what I tried to achieve, to expose these scoundrels, to stop their cheating."

"There were election meetings last night organised by your political opponents. They read out your whole letter, to stir up people against you, raising their ire."

"That's what I had warned you about, Bernie," Harriet commented. "What you wrote harms not only the rogues, but also the honest miners who want to float their companies to raise money for expansion, or just to keep going."

"Anyway," Louis continued urgently. "There are hundreds of people milling around Clarke Street, saying you defamed Hill End and you ruined the goldfields. More angry men are arriving from neighbouring towns. They're slowly moving this way. Somebody brought a scarecrow to represent you and they're throwing rotten fruit at it."

"They are coming here?" Harriet asked, picking up little Sophia. "What shall we do?"

"Yes, they're on their way," Louis confirmed. "They want to tar and feather you, Bernhardt!"

"What the hell, I'm not afraid. I'll talk to them and explain how things have got out of hand lately."

"What if they won't let you talk?" Harriet urged him while she was putting a few essentials into a travelling bag.

"Yes, Bernhardt," Louis agreed with Harriet. "They are saying you are begrudging others making money. You must leave." Louis looked nervously out the window. "I spoke with Moses Bell. He is bringing his carriage to the back lane behind your house. Get ready quickly."

"Let's go to my parents in Bathurst," Harriet suggested. "We can stay there, till this blows over."

Bernhardt and Harriet grabbed some belongings and bundled up their little girl. Yelling and screaming could now be heard outside the house. A rock smashed through a window. "Traitor, traitor," chanted angry voices.

Louis held the back door open. They saw the rear of the waiting carriage. Bernhardt pressed Louis' arm on the way out. "Thanks, Louis. You are a true friend. I really appreciate your concern. Keep the mine roster running while I'm away. It'll be just a few days."

The family of three scrambled into the carriage and off they went, unnoticed by the growing crowd out the front.

A few minutes later, Louis Beyers opened the front door and stepped outside. "The Holtermanns are not here," he announced. "They have gone to Gulgong."

Agitators were still stirring up the mass of people moving from Clarke Street past Holtermann's house to the edge of town, as the crowd followed the straw dummy representing Holtermann. Accompanied by cheering and swearing, Holtermann's effigy was burnt on a nearby hill.

⚜

After Moses Bell had inconspicuously returned with his carriage to Hill End, Mark Hammond came to ask him for his help.

Hammond explained, "James Brown, or Northumberland Jimmy, as they call him, is returning to England."

"Yes, I understand he's made enough money in his many years here. He's cleaning up his affairs."

"He's also selling his share in the Star of Hope. He's asking five hundred pounds for it. I'd really be interested in a stake in the mine, but right now I don't have the money. That's why I am here, Moses, to see if you'd help me out with a loan."

"Well, it would certainly be good to have you as a partner in the Star of Hope. We need your prospecting expertise. There are rich veins being discovered all around us, but not on our claim. Perhaps we've dug too deep. That's what Edwards is saying. He's just become a new member of the syndicate. You'd be the man to assess the operation to see whether it can be improved."

"I have the same feeling as Edwards. There must be good reefs in there. That's why I want to become a partner. But Holtermann is the mine manager. We'd have to convince him if we want to change the approach."

"Yes, Mark, we'll see about that. Talk it over with Edwards first."

"The other problem is, I can't start working the claim myself, immediately. I still have other commitments. In a few months I'll be able to take up my shifts and start my evaluation. In the meantime I can let my off-sider work on wages."

"Start as early as possible. I'm glad you want to come on board. I'll lend you the money. I have the feeling it'll be a good investment for both of us."

"Great. I'll go and tell Brown immediately that I'll buy his share before someone else snaps it up. Everybody and his dog are going crazy about investment in goldmining these days."

They laughed. Hammond shook Bell's hand and thanked him as he left.

In Bathurst, the Emmett family was happy to have their daughter at home for a while, but centre stage was stolen by little Sophia. Her grandparents were amazed how smart and advanced the girl was for her age. She kept everybody busy and entertained. On the other hand, Mrs Emmett was less than pleased about her son-in-law, whom she liked as a person with his variety of interests, but she was certainly not impressed by his financial misfortunes and his inability to support his young family.

"How can you manage at all?" she asked Harriet. "You were not so frugal before your marriage."

"I know mother, I didn't really appreciate the value of things. Now that I have to do without, I see how spoilt I was. But I'm not complaining. I'm happy with Bernie, even if his luck's down right now. The goldfields are booming and I'm sure we'll get our share of the riches."

Harriet turned her attention to Sophia as Mrs Emmett looked on, admiring her granddaughter.

"Does he have any income at all, your Bernie?"

"Not now. We got some lump sums when we took three minor partners into the syndicate. That was shortly after the mine accident. The blasting revealed a bit of gold then, but since then it has been a poor showing. The money's used up. We had to pay a miner while Bernie couldn't work. The rest we spent little by little. Now we get our basic groceries from Chan on charge. He's the only one who still gives us credit at Hill End."

"Your father could advance you a bit of money, dear."

"No, thanks. I'm sure Bernie wouldn't take it."

"Perhaps you needn't even tell him."

"No, mother, I couldn't do that, not behind his back. I wouldn't only compromise his pride, but also my loyalty."

Mr Emmett and Bernhardt entered the room in conversation.

Mrs Emmett turned to them, saying, "Harriet and I were just talking about your financial difficulties, Bernhardt. Harriet is so sweet, she refuses to complain about the situation. I didn't imagine she'd make such a strong and loyal wife."

"You're right. Things haven't turned out as well as we thought at the time of our wedding," Bernhardt conceded. "I don't know how I could've come through these terrible times without Harriet." He embraced his wife. "At least I have my health back. But now, not only are we down on money, on top of it everybody at Hill End seems to hate me for that letter I wrote."

Turning to Mr Emmett he explained, "They are hypocrites. Most of them know I am right. While I'm here, I'm going to write a letter to the *Hill End and Tambaroora Times*. I'll challenge everyone to be specific and deny the truth of what I wrote in the *Sydney Morning Herald*. When I go back to Hill End, I'll parade down Clarke Street with my head held high." And turning to Mrs Emmett again, Bernhardt smiled, "After all, I almost got elected to Parliament. I just missed by five votes, imagine that, by five votes. Only because of the circus about my letter. Next time I'll be elected for sure."

He smiled at his wife. "Harriet, you'll be the wife of an eminent politician and of a successful goldminer."

"And much more," she replied. "We'll travel the world with your photographic exhibition. We'll be Australia's greatest promoters."

Mr Emmett nodded his head and smiled. "We were just talking outside. You could be rich even now, whether you find gold or not, if Bernhardt swallows his pride and acts contrary to his own advice."

"Not exactly against my advice," Bernhardt corrected. "In my letter I was warning against unsubstantiated investment and speculation in fictitious or useless mine sites. Our Star of Hope claim is well established for close to a decade. It's already once produced substantial findings, and enough since to remain promising, especially with all the gold veins being unearthed around us."

"Nevertheless, if you want to float your mine as publicly traded stock, it's as well to keep the frenzy up, even if it is irrational in some areas. It's up to the greedy investor what he wants to buy and how much he knows about a specific offering. New shares of some Hill End mines have been floated in Sydney recently for more than a hundred thousand pounds. Imagine such amounts, if you will! You could buy all of Bathurst for that money."

"The reason why I didn't consider turning our syndicate into a stock company was that I was afraid I would lose control with so many new shareholders coming in. But after discussing all the pros and cons with you, it is now clear to me that the current partners would still be commanding stock holders. The difference is that we would own our part of the mine in the form of publicly traded shares that have monetary value and can be sold for cash, or be borrowed on. We get our shares without paying since we have set up the company and made it worth investing in. New shareholders will have to buy their stocks, giving the mine extra operating capital. They buy on the expectation that we will find more gold. My partners and I will be rich instantly, as long as the positive outlook for our shares remains."

"And if you find gold, the stocks go up and you are even richer," Mr Emmett emphasised. Mrs Emmett looked puzzled. "You mean they can get real money, right now?"

"Yes, dear," Mr Emmett explained. "Say the stock market float goes for seventy-five thousand pounds. Bernhardt might own stocks to the value of twenty-five thousand pounds. That's more than a lifetime's income. He can sell a few shares for cash. If he thinks there'll be no gold in the mine ever, he can cash them all in."

"No, I won't do that," Bernhardt protested. "I still want to be a major beneficiary when we strike it rich at the claim." He looked proudly around the room. "I'm sure Louis will have no objection to the public share offer if I explain it to him the way we discussed it here. Then I'll have to go to Sydney to get everything organised. Lloyd stock brokers have an agent at Hill End. I'll talk to him first."

"I was just reading," Mr Emmett mentioned, "that they are planning to set up a proper Stock Exchange in Sydney now, the Royal Exchange in Bridge Street. So far, brokers traded shares in Hayes Coffee House in Pitt Street, and in teashops and hotels."

Bernhardt picked up little Sophia and carried her over to Harriet. "Wouldn't it be wonderful if we could visit Sydneytown together after all these years? Perhaps we can leave Sophia here for a few weeks."

Mrs Emmett was delighted. "Of course you can," she answered even before being asked.

Mr Emmett nodded contentedly. "You must go together," he agreed. "I can see clearly how the brokers will fall all over each other to get their hands onto a well established mine like the Star of Hope."

Bernhardt made his plans. "I'll first make contact with agents at Hill End. They can organise our trip and put us up in a nice hotel in Sydney. A bit of advance cash as a retainer would help, too. The Hamburg Hotel will not be good enough, but we'll visit Müller there, Harriet, for old time's sake!"

"Mother," beamed Harriet, "did you hear that? Real riches await us, just for the taking. Hill End is booming and we profit from it. Now we're at the right place at the right time. We had it hard for so many years. We deserve a fortune."

Mrs Emmett embraced her daughter. Bernhardt put his arms around both ladies.

Mr Emmett smiled slyly. "I have some champagne put away for special occasions," he announced. "I guess they don't come more special than this. You visiting us, Harriet, with your beautiful child and your husband, and now Bernhardt's decision to go public with the mine. Let me fetch the bottle. Harriet, get the glasses, dear."

※

After offering the agents their company for a stock market float, the Holtermanns were treated royally by the brokers. All partners received their share of a retainer fee. Bernhardt and Harriet were escorted on the daily coach to Wallerowany and from there first class on the new train to Sydney. In the city Harriet was invited on a shopping trip while Bernhardt provided the facts and figures and the marketing script for the share prospectus. He was taken to elegant city clubs. The couple was wined and dined, taken to shows and invited to the private viewing boxes at the races and the cricket. Having always felt like an entrepreneur, Bernhardt enjoyed his new role as corporate promoter. Harriet slipped into her newly elevated position in life with charm and intelligence.

Returning to their opulent hotel room one evening, Bernhardt had a broad smile for Harriet. "Tomorrow we'll have two things to celebrate," he announced, "our fourth wedding anniversary and the full subscription to our public share offer. The company has been successfully floated."

The couple embraced and kissed with newfound passion.

"I hope we won't see four years like that again," Harriet mused. "You hanging between life and death, me reduced to buying food on credit."

There was a knock on the door and as a waiter delivered and uncorked a bottle of champagne, the couple had time to clear their minds of the lingering memories of those past years, the losses on the two mines, the miscarriage, the mining accident, the death of their four weeks old son, and just recently the lost election and the town's hateful reaction to Bernhardt's letter to the newspaper. The waiter left with a bow.

"How quickly things have changed to quite the opposite

end of the spectrum," Bernhardt marvelled. "We are incredibly rich now," he said jubilantly, embracing Harriet. They held each other in warm embrace. "We certainly were down, but never out."

"The main thing is," Harriet smiled, "we stuck through it with each other."

"And we have a healthy daughter to show for it," Bernhardt beamed.

"One daughter is a good beginning, but one is certainly not enough," Harriet hinted. "The time has never been better."

As Bernhardt made himself comfortable holding a glass of champagne he enjoyed watching Harriet how she playfully removed the elaborate layers of her street dress and underclothing to put on no more than her red morning gown.

Harriet and Bernhardt were unaware that, in the busy harbour near their hotel, a tall ship from London had tied up that day. In the first class section an officer had arrived, a new aide to the Governor. He had brought with him his wife, two children, and their governess, Victoria. The elegant family, but particularly the young governess, had turned heads as they walked off the ship and made their entrance into the city. Victoria was in her first employment after finishing at her exclusive boarding school in England. She had accepted the position even though the children would not require her tuition any longer in one or two years time. She would not have missed this opportunity to see the world for anything.

1872

REEF MINING

Bernhardt was back at the Star of Hope Mine at Hawkins Hill outside the town of Hill End. From the fancy city suit and top hat, he was back into his well worn miners' outfit. He stood on the heap of rocks that surrounded the mouth of the shaft, after having hoisted up the last bucket of quartz and slate. Bernhardt gave the whip horse one final spur for this shift, getting it to walk its circles under the sheltering roof. The horse pulled up the one remaining load from the bottom of the shaft hundreds of feet below –the miner who had been chiseling away at the rock for hours by the light of the candle. Louis was glad to see daylight again, see his partner, the horse, and not least the green bush surrounding them.

"Nothing but mullock," Bernhardt lamented, talking of the day's results.

"I know, not a trace of gold in it. No fiery glitter in the reflections of the candle down there. How I long for that sight," Louis smiled bitterly as he slapped dirt and dust off his clothing.

Edwards and Hunt arrived for the evening shift.

"No encouraging results so far," Bernhardt reported to them. "We are not deep enough yet."

"I have to talk to you and Louis about that," replied Edwards. "We could go deeper, till the cows come home and still hit no gold. There's hardly any shaft deeper than ours here on the hill. Mark Hammond and I've studied the veins that have been discovered around us and I've come to the conclusion that we need to drive a horizontal shaft to the west at one hundred and thirty feet below the surface."

"Are you serious?" Bernhardt protested. "Are you saying

that we've put in years of effort to go down four hundred feet, only to look now for a reef at hundred and thirty? We would've done years of backbreaking work for nothing." Bernhardt shook his head in angry disbelief. "Of course, that doesn't worry you. You weren't part of that struggle. You didn't risk your life in an explosion to drive that shaft down. I did."

"It was no waste, it was exploration. Now we know there's nothing there at lower levels. Without going down, we wouldn't have known. We learnt from it. Now Mark and I are convinced higher up will be more promising."

"We already went through that hundred and thirty foot level. There's no reef there."

"Yes, not exactly where you went down, but the claim is wider. We have to dig sideways."

"Dig sideways? What an idea! You do that only after you cross a vein, to follow it."

Now Edwards got angry too. "You're so smart, Bernhardt. How come you haven't found any gold for years if you're so smart? The mines I've been involved with have all done better."

"Are you saying you want to take over the running of this claim now?"

"It'd probably be better, since you don't seem to know what you're doing. For one, it'd be more efficient to work closer to the surface."

Bernhardt's face was reddening with anger. "I'm the mine manager," he bellowed. "Let me make this very clear. We do what I say."

"I do have the support of Moses Bell and of Mark Hammond for this plan," Edwards insisted.

"I see, you have been plotting against me, you mongrel. That'll get you nowhere. All your shares put together count nothing against mine."

"Who are you calling a mongrel, you pompous little

showoff? Why don't you learn to pronounce our English language properly before you bully everybody around?"

Bernhardt lunged at Edwards. "You arrogant English bastard. I never invited you into our syndicate. You bought your way in on the sly, you devious scoundrel."

Edwards grabbed Bernhardt. "I'll break your neck," Edwards yelled. "I came in because I knew there had to be gold on this claim, and now you ignorant bastard, you won't let me get to it."

"Let go of me," Bernhardt hissed as he reached back and pulled a knife from his belt. "Here, have this, you stupid ass."

In the nick of time Louis and Hunt jumped in and pulled the two men apart.

Bernhardt fumed. "You have nothing to say here, Edwards. You're just a minority partner. As mine manager I've decided to sink the shaft deeper, and that's exactly what you'll do. It's your shift. Don't waste any more time!"

Bernhardt stamped off the site. Hunt shook his fist after him. Louis exchanged a few consoling words with Edwards, then he followed Bernhardt. Dejected and enraged Edwards and Hunt started work.

Another week passed. Edwards and Hunt arrived for their shift again. As soon as the others had disappeared over the hill, Hammond joined them. He explained his plan to Hunt.

"Today is the day," he said. "We'll have to do it without their consent. We don't want to waste our time and effort on hopeless digging, do we?"

"Of course not," Hunt agreed. "Why dig further away from where you say the reef must be? Anyway, you're the boss."

"Right, here's what we'll do. The most important task is to timber off the shaft at the right level in a way that'll make it virtually impossible to remove the blockage. Then the other work shifts will have no alternative but to follow our tunnel. After we've built a secure blockage, we'll work like the devil to drive the horizontal shaft west as far as possible. Can I rely on you to give it all you've got today?"

"Yes, Sir, we'll show them. We'll dig like mad."

"All right, friends, let's get the timber. I'll go below first. Ease me down to a hundred and thirty. I'll prepare for the support structure. Later we'll take turns."

The three shook hands. "Here's to our luck," Edwards smiled. "If we're wrong, we'll be in a hell of a strife!"

At the end of the shift, the three men were exhausted. They had little fight left in them when Holtermann and Beyers arrived for the next shift. Edwards just informed them of the change as a *fait accompli*. In disbelief Holtermann went below to inspected the blockage. When he returned to the surface he was absolutely furious.

"How can you ruin eight years work?" he cried. "We started this mine and we sunk every penny we had into it. Now you have forever ruined any chances to make this claim pay. Or have you found any gold in your new tunnel?"

"Not yet," Edwards conceded. "We worked on it only for a few hours, not years, as you did in your shaft."

"I had expressly forbidden you to start a horizontal drive. This is an atrocity the likes of which Hill End has never seen. Our shaft blocked for ever! The Star of Hope Mine ruined. I can't express my outrage. But I'll let my deeds speak for me. I swear I'll never lift a finger to work in that new drive."

Beyers agreed with his old friend and the two of them left the mine site in a helpless fuming rage.

For the time being Bernhardt was disillusioned with mining. He thought of selling his shares while their value was still up and getting out of the gold business all together. With his wealth from the stock market he felt a bit strange anyway, still going down the dark, narrow shaft, doing back breaking, dirty and dangerous work in that dreadful isolation from the world above. How much more gentlemanly was photography, with its exciting new technology, chemistry and artistry. It could produce real magic. He had always remembered it fondly from his days in Sydney. Bernhardt noticed that a professional photographer had recently set up business at Hill End. Henry Beaufoy Merlin advertised the services of his American and Australasian Photographic Company in the *Hill End and Tambaroora Times*. Bernhardt now saw an opportunity to further his dream of popularising Australia overseas with impressive photographs. He met with Merlin.

Merlin was a tall, hawk-faced man without the customary beard, sporting only a wide moustache. Holtermann would have taken him for an English lord, not the artistic entrepreneur he was.

The business card of the photographic company depicted the achievements of modern times, a railway steam engine with a tall chimney blowing a plume of smoke, and a large sailing ship featuring a billowing smokestack among its rigging.

Bernhardt agreed to finance an initial production of two large panoramic depictions of the great reefing area along the western slope of Hawkins Hill. With his local connections he helped organise the bush carpenters to construct a tall, steady platform in a clearing high on the opposite ridge. Merlin selected his special long distance optics. The big camera for large glassplate negatives had to be brought in along a rough track together with the horse drawn laboratory caravan. Any glass negative needed to be the same size as the picture that would be produced from it. For large photographs the camera had to be of sufficient size to accommodate glassplate negatives of equally large dimensions. Only small plates were available commercially. Large negatives were hand coated in the laboratory caravan where the exposures were also transferred to photographic paper and chemically developed. The journey, setting up, preparation and execution of photographs took several days.

Returning from the photographic expedition, Bernhardt was greeted with amazing and exciting news. The Star of Hope Mine had hit the richest gold reef ever uncovered at Hill End. After working the horizontal shaft by themselves for a week, Edwards, Hammond and Hunt had struck a bonanza. The first quartz crushing at the stamper battery yielded well over 1000 ounces of gold. The news spread like bushfire all over Australia. Goldmining stocks hit a new high, led by Star of Hope shares.

Bernhardt was glad he had not had time to seriously consider selling his stocks. With so much wealth going around amongst the partners, the disagreement between the various shifts working the mine was quickly forgotten. Nobody thought of digging deeper anymore. With constant rewards of more glittering finds, everybody worked the horizontal drives with excitement and vigour. Further goldbearing veins cut across the extent of the claim. Specimens were exhibited in a secure shop window at Hill End, eliciting envy and greed in the eyes of admirers. Photographs were taken for the newspapers, displaying large jagged lumps of reef gold set out on tables, flanked by various members of the syndicate, from Holtermann and Beyers to Hammond, Bell and Edwards. Bearded men in dark hats, their faces stern and proud.

1872

ENDLESS RICHES

Bernhardt was leaving the new mine office he had set up, having instructed the clerk to keep detailed records of all activities, from the ongoing sale of gold to the bank after crushing, to operating expenses and work rosters. He was proud that more than a dozen people were now directly associated with the running of the mine. He had recognised early on that this required orderly planning and control of operations and of monetary dealings. Passing the bank on Clark Street, Bernhardt mused about the incredible amounts of money which were now regularly flowing into his personal account. Most of the company's vast income was paid out in dividends, set by the syndicate and reported to the stock exchange in Sydney. The majority of dividends flowed back to Bernhardt and Louis. The high level of dividends enticed more investors, who were attracted by the appealing price to earnings ratio. The strong demand for the stock increased its value more and more. Bernhardt smiled at his fortune of still being the largest share holder.

Before he reached home, he dropped in at the coachbuilder's shop, where he was greeted with respect by Mr Moller.

"The buggy we imported for you from America will be ready tomorrow. Its all unpacked and assembled. All we have to do now is polish it up. It will be the most fashionable we have ever sold."

"I hope so. I have already bought a pair of dapplegrey stallions for it. They will be a handful to control. That's why I hired Ashold, my Oriental groom. He has a way with horses."

"You'll cut the finest figure around town!" Moller ingratiated himself.

"I may even go as far as Sydney in the buggy, to get people to invest into my new shops I have built here. We should make a good impression in Sydney, too."

"Certainly," Moller smiled. "We are all very proud of you and how you get things moving around here. You are the toast of our town and an inspiration to us all, Mr Holtermann."

"Well, thank you for saying so." Holtermann bowed and waved farewell. "I'll let Ashold know to get the buggy tomorrow then."

Returning home, Bernhardt found their little house crowded. Harriet was busy with the maid and the seamstress. A nursemaid was looking after Sophia as the little girl tried her first steps.

"How is our princess today?" Bernhardt inquired as he picked up his daughter, lifting her up toward the rafters. She wriggled and screamed with joy. After swinging her through the air a few times, Bernhardt gave her back to the nursemaid.

Harriet retreated with her husband to the bedroom where they had privacy for a warm embrace.

"Our dream has come true with a vengeance," Bernhardt beamed at Harriet. "We are richer than we ever had expected to be. We've not only found gold, but we reap stock market windfalls as well. Whatever happens, we'll never be poor again. Now we have more money than we ever can spend." Harriet poured two glasses of sherry. "The best," she smiled, "all the way from Spain." She raised her glass. "To you, Bernie. Your persistence has paid off. So many years of sacrifice and hard work."

He shook his head slowly, his mind wandering back. "But the smartest decision was yours, my love, not to sell our majority share when our luck seemed to sour, when I was flat on my back, just as you were carrying our first baby."

"Well, we've had a few false starts and a long drought, but that's over now." Harriet sat down on the bed. "Sophia is doing well. Now we can truly afford a big family," Harriet contemplated, "with servants to help me bringing up the children properly, and with money for the best education. But there's only so much we can do here at Hill End. And the house is so small. Let's make plans. Now you can turn all your dreams into reality, Bernie."

"I'm doing that already. I've contracted Merlin to produce a series of photographs of our prosperous mining towns. He'll start in Hill End, taking large pictures of the mines, of each shop and establishment, together with their owners, perhaps adding some panoramas of the town and of our street life, and then he'll do the same at Gulgong. Next I'll send him to your home town, my dear, and on to Rockley, to Montefiores and to Orange."

"These pictures will show the world how organised and civilised our 'frontier life' is."

"Yes, indeed. But we'll also tackle the big cities. Perhaps I can get Merlin and his laboratory to Melbourne to capture the grandeur of that metropolis. Can you imagine it on our silver plates?" he glowed. "And finally we'll be on to Sydney, capturing its wooded hills rolling down to the bay, Port Jackson, the harbour at Walsh Bay crammed with tall ships from around the world, the mansions in their tropical gardens, the bustling city streets, George, Pitt, and elegant Macquarie."

"I know you love your Sydneytown," Harriet smiled. "It'll be a good place to bring up the children. And I know you can't wait for us to live there. That shouldn't be too far off now that you have paid labour working the mine for you."

"Well, I'm still the mine manager. But you are right, now we could raise our children anywhere in the world, London, Hamburg, New York. To some extent we could buy our way into society anywhere, but Sydney will do me fine. Our children will have the best of everything there and they'll grow up with the right perspective on life. My heart is in Australia. This country has been really good to me. I belong here. I like you Australian folk, my dear Harriet." He squeezed her arm, remembering suddenly what a daring gesture this had been when they first had met. "You are a reasonable lot. I can see my purpose in being here. There are many things I can do for this country."

"Why don't you try running for Parliament again? You were so close last time. In Parliament you'll be able to help set the right framework for economic growth and prosperity."

"Yes, Parliament is already on my list. Then there is the photographic exposition we can take overseas, and there will be our mansion on the hill, and business ventures I have in mind. You can see I've got a lot to do." He appreciated Harriet's belief in him and the enthusiasm they shared. "I'll repay this country as much as I can for the opportunities and the happiness I've found here."

"You sound as if you were already practising your speeches for the election campaign, dear. I like you a lot when you get carried away like that." She shook her head and smiled. "And I thought we might take it easy for a while, now that we can afford it, travel the world and live royally."

"Taking it easy is not my style, but travelling and living royally sounds good to me, too. There's plenty of time to fit it all in, but we'll do it with a purpose in mind."

Harriet had been listening, but she was waiting for an opportunity to make her own announcement. "Talking of the future, Bernie," she mused, "I think I'll soon be certain of some good news."

"What good news? Anything related to the household?"

"Oh, you men! Much more important than that."

Seeing his puzzled look, she put his hand on her stomach.

"Are you saying we can expect another baby?" he beamed.

"It's looked like it for a few weeks now."

They embraced again and kissed. Bernhardt couldn't have been more pleased.

"If it's a son, let's call him Sydney," he blurted out.

"And how about Esther for a girl?"

"Why not? We'll see, my love." He put his arm around Harriet. "Whatever we plan now, we have to think about you and our children first. We have to get you to Sydney where you can get the best accommodation and the best care. As soon as I can, I'll follow you. We'll set up a proper household there. And then we'll build our fine home on a hill in North Sydney."

"But don't you have to supervise the business here, love?"

"Yes, for a while. But we must be realistic, at the rate we are mining now, we'll have exhausted all possible veins in a few short years. Everybody is euphoric now, but in two years most of the gold will be depleted."

"So you have to sell your shares before business declines."

"You are not just a picturebook beauty! You are right, my dear. When the stock market goes crazy and everybody and his dog wants to get his share of rocketing fortunes, we'll sell out quietly. I have a pretty good idea how long the mines around here will yield gold. I'm a few steps ahead of the average investor who follows the mindless frenzy of the press. Many of them will lose their money regardless of what we do with our shares. I tried to warn them once and almost got lynched. That taught me a lesson. You can't help gamblers and starry-eyed speculators."

"Yes, we know it well. It takes years of preparation to create an overnight success!" Harriet pronounced theatrically.

He laughed and nodded. "Persistence is important, but when circumstances change we do need to be flexible."

Harriet smiled wistfully. "Hill End's been nice, despite the hard times. We've made some good friends here. I'll never forget the dances at the hotels."

The traditional quadrille, danced collectively, had always provided a pleasant opportunity to walk and talk with friends during the half hour sequence. And lately they had even swung to the new waltz, which allowed people to get heartwarmingly close to each other.

"We were always well respected," Harriet continued, "and now new arrivals to the town revere us as the epitome of successful old-timers."

"The town's bursting at the seams," Bernhardt nodded. "Tens of thousands of people from all over the world. It's good for business. I am buying into some more enterprises. Have I told you? Like our new newspaper, the *Hill End Observer*. It's a boom now, but this'll become a ghost town in no time, once gold runs out."

"What will happen to the people who are here then?" Harriet wondered. She remembered how Hill End had grown from a sleepy settlement into a town of bustling commerce. On the hills many of the trees had been hewn for steam generation to drive the stamper batteries that ground on day and night. Their din and other mining commotion made it hard to sleep. Miners returned from late shifts at all hours of the night, and the coach for Bathurst left the inn noisily at four in the morning. In addition to the pandemonium, there was the constant dust in summer. If there was no dust, people were wading in mud.

"Lets drink to the elegant life in the big city," Harriet cheered with her refilled glass.

"To Sydney!" Bernhardt raised his glass. "And I'll help it grow. I'll invest my money there and start new businesses. That's the place to be. There we can go to the theatres and the balls and enjoy the city's culture."

"All right, Bernie, I'll make plans to move then. I'll ask the nursemaid to come along to look after Sophia. We'll go to Bathurst first. I am sure Mother will come along to Sydney and help me get started. We'll book into a hotel or guesthouse and then I'll start looking for a house to rent. Only the best will do, am I right, Bernie?" They smiled at each other in anticipation and kissed tenderly.

After dinner Bernhardt went to the 'Manchester Unity Independent Order of Odd-Fellows, Lodge No. 47, Loyal United Miners' where he was awarded a medal for his contributions to the lodge and to the prosperity of Hill End. There were speeches and jovial verbal roasting. Bernhardt returned home late. Sleepily he flipped the calendar leaf to the next day before going to bed. The print on the stack of leaves read 19 October 1872.

The night shift was still at work at the Star of Hope. At two in the morning the last charge was exploded in a horizontal drive to leave work ready for the morning crew, but Hunt was too curious to leave without inspecting the result. As he was winched up again and approached the top of the shaft, his workmates heard him screaming. They were concerned he might be injured. But when they saw his excited face appear at the top of the shaft, they knew better.

"Gold, gold, gold," he bellowed. "A whole wall of it. Nothing but yellow glitter, the entire end of the tunnel, one shining, sparkling mass of gold."

He fell into the arms of his mates. They all cheered and slapped each other on the back, sending the dust flying in the moonlit night.

"I can't wait to break it all up and hoist the pieces into daylight. What a sight for sore eyes that will be!"

The others wanted to see the golden wall for themselves and hurriedly helped each other down the shaft.

Hunt ran, more than walked to the Holtermanns' house. Regardless of the hour he knew that the mine manager wanted to be informed of such an event.

Bernhardt thought he was dreaming in his first deep sleep

when he heard knocking and calling at his door. Since the maid didn't live with them, Harriet shook Bernhardt awake. He finally woke up to open the door to an elated Hunt.

"We blasted out the largest mass of gold I have ever seen. One continuous stretch, many feet long," Hunt reported loudly. "It was our final charge for the night. Who knows how deep it runs in the vein? A whole wall of gold."

Bernhardt listened and slowly came to his senses. He hesitated before he spoke. Gold, more gold, he thought. Perhaps it wasn't time yet to leave this place.

"That's incredible, Hunt. Good work. This'll be something for the newspapers again to go crazy about," he laughed. He considered how to maximise the publicity. "Do you think we can get a huge nugget out in one piece?"

"We've never done that before. We've always brought up manageable pieces. The reef needs to be broken up below."

"Well, not this one. We'll have to talk about it in the morning. We'll keep the largest possible block we can get through the shaft. We're making history here, mate. We need something we can show to the world. I might even buy the specimen myself as a showpiece for my Australian exhibition."

"It won't be easy, but you are the mine manager. Whatever you say, boss."

"Yes, I'll be there at the start of the next shift to make sure no damage will be done to our nugget. Thanks for the news. It's great. There'll be a special bonus to all workers if we get this one out intact. How exciting, Hunt!"

He said goodnight and left Hunt to celebrate the find with his workmates. Once inside, Bernhardt told Harriet the news. They talked for a while. After that they were too thrilled to sleep again.

But Bernhardt wasn't tired the next morning at the early shift. When he came up the shaft after his inspection he threw up his arms in excitement.

"It's incredible," he beamed at the growing assembly of

miners. "A sheer stretch of golden glitter. Hill End, we love you!"

As the others cheered, Bernhardt stood aside for a moment, overcome by emotions. His old boyhood emotion about gold hit him with force. The exuberance was too much to bear, bringing tears to his eyes. Wasn't it absolutely amazing how things had turned out? But he didn't have time for reverie. He gathered his wits and blew his nose. Going back to the others, he gave his instructions to the shift going down.

"Make sure you break a single block from the matrix as wide as the shaft permits and as long as possible. The quartz is brittle, so be careful how it breaks. You've got so little room to work in. Secure the line extra carefully. We don't want to drop the damn thing on the way up and smash it to pieces."

When the jagged lump of gold-bearing quartz was finally hoisted clear of the shaft, foot by foot rising into the sunlight, glistening taller and taller, the miners stood in awe. Again, Bernhardt had tears in his eyes and his voice broke as he gave further instructions.

"Right, men. Let's put these six crowbars on the ground and tilt the nugget slowly across them. Twelve men should be able to carry the block to the top of the ridge. There we'll have a horse cart waiting to take it to town." Recovering control he added, "We'll have the treasure weighed and measured. And we'll take some pictures. Merlin is our man for that."

Hunt crowed his latest information. "I heard another photographer from Beavis Brothers is already rushing here from Bathurst to get pictures for the papers. We'll all be famous!"

Before carrying it away the workmates examined the giant block of gold and quartz in amazement, almost intoxicated by the extraordinary sight, raving with enthusiasm as they guessed the size and weight of the golden rock.

Louis Beyers rarely left Hill End, but this special day he

and Mary were enjoying their new wealth, away on a trip. Alfred Bullock was replacing him at the mine.

For the official photograph, the giant nugget was propped up on end. Everybody available from the Star of Hope syndicate massed around it, seventeen men altogether. Holtermann sat next to the towering specimen on one side, Bullock on the other, surrounded by other partners, with workmates beside and behind them.

"Don't move for three seconds," the photographer reminded them. "If you do, your image will be blurred. Ready, now, twenty-one, twenty-two, twenty-three. Thank you, gentlemen."

Holtermann stepped forward. "Let's just take one picture of me alone with the nugget," he told the photographer.

"Why's that?" asked Bullock. "You didn't find it. It belongs to all of us."

"I would actually like to buy it," Holtermann countered, "to preserve it as an exhibition item."

Edwards joined the conversation. "You want all the glory, Bernhardt, but this find is based on my expertise. You know very well we are getting all the gold in the horizontal tunnels which you resisted even by pulling your knife on me."

Bell and Hammond agreed with Edwards's objections.

"We've never sold any specimens," commented Bell. "It is difficult to assess the value. We don't know how much of it is gold and how much is quartz. We'll only know after the separation at the stamper mill."

"It's also risky to leave the gold lying around," added Hammond. "We have no safe storage. It's better to get to the stamper fast and to lodge the gold with the bank. Then we have the money in the company's account."

Bullock made a practical proposal. "There is a crushing going on right now. We could still include the rock. If we miss it we'll have to store the nugget until the next crushing. I say we take it to the stamper right now."

Bell, Hammond and Edwards agreed.

"Right," nodded Holtermann. "It could be awkward and risky to keep the nugget, and it is difficult to move it around. Let's get it crushed. But we must take at least one closeup picture of the specimen alone. Photographer", he waved, "come closer. Take the nugget by itself, with the clear sky behind it. A real monument to all our efforts and to our common success."

Merlin placed his unwieldy tripod with the bulky camera in front of the nugget and exposed his plate.

A few days after the find, Bernhardt went to the photographic studio where he saw Merlin and his young assistant, Charles Bayliss, who had joined him from Melbourne. Bernhardt unwrapped some pictures and glass negatives he had brought along.

"The newspapers are asking for photographs of our giant specimen," he explained. "I don't like the picture with the whole assembly of people around it. The nugget appears insignificant between them. The picture of the rock alone doesn't give any perspective of its size either. Now that the specimen has been crushed, we can't take any new pictures. Anyway, if we call it the Holtermann Nugget, we should have a photograph of me standing beside it. Can you gentlemen produce a photomontage?"

"Of course," nodded Merlin. "We just take a picture of you and join it with the one of the nugget alone. We can do it now. Let's take the camera outside behind the house to a sunny spot. Charles, get some plates."

Bernhardt was pleased. "Right, I'll take my coat off and turn up my sleeves. Should I sit or stand?"

"If you sit, the nugget will be taller than you, if you stand, it will be almost the same height."

"Standing is better. Or we could produce a picture with me putting my arm around the rock of gold."

"Perhaps you could just rest your arm on the nugget. That'd be easier to assemble. Look here, on the picture of the specimen there is a shoulder not far from the top. That would be the best place to put your hand. It would be about four or five feet from the ground. To touch that you'll be standing to the left. Can you hold your right hand at that height?"

"I might not be able to hold it still for a few seconds."

"Yes, you are right. Charles, we need an object four to five feet high for Mr Holtermann to rest his hand on. See what you can find inside."

Charles returned with a hat stand. "This is ideal," he smiled contentedly. "It has a steady foot like a tripod and even a straight handle on top."

"Perfect," laughed Bernhardt. Then he became serious to pose with a sombre expression for the photograph, resting one hand on the hat stand, the other on his hip.

Merlin bent down to the camera and stuck his head under the black cloth at the back. "Ready," he called out. "One, two, three."

They changed the glass plate at the rear of the camera. "Let's take a few more shots. This time, look to your right, Mr Holtermann."

Eventually Merlin was satisfied. "We should have the montage finished this afternoon," he promised.

"I am looking forward to see it." Bernhardt smiled as he pronounced theatrically, "Mr Holtermann and his gold nugget. The largest specimen of reef gold in the world!"

1873

SYDNEY

On New Year's Day 1873, in brilliant summer weather, the foundation-laying ceremony was held for a new Hill End public hospital. Despite Bernhardt's belief that the gold would run out and the town would decline, he had seized the opportunity to support the hospital, since he wanted to express his gratitude to Hill End and participate in a project that would always benefit the wider district. Louis Beyers had just become mayor of Hill End and he was particularly pleased by Bernhardt's contribution.

For the ceremony a small podium had been built on the side of a hill in a clearing at the edge of town and a lectern had been placed on it to allow for the official addresses. Louis introduced Bernhardt as one of the speakers.

"And who would be more appropriate to address us on an occasion like this than my old friend, our revered Mr Bernhardt Holtermann. His generous financial contribution makes the construction of a solid, stone built hospital possible. But besides that, he is a man who has experienced the ups and downs of life at Hill End for almost a decade, and he has come out on top. After arriving as a penniless immigrant from Germany, he has created one of the most successful mining companies in Australia. He and his venerable wife started their family here in town, and they have made good friends not only at Hill End, but also in the city of Sydney. Please welcome a man who knows life, who knows us, and who knows the world!"

Holtermann was greeted with applause as he stepped to the lectern.

"Esteemed officials, dear friends. Thank you for your generous introduction, Mr Mayor. As was mentioned, I came here from Germany many years back. And I am glad I did for several reasons. In the meantime Germany has been at war with France. The reason I left was mainly to escape the draft. Imagine, they would've had their war while I was in the army. That the Germans won is neither here nor there. I would've stood a good chance of being killed in the process. I could've done nothing for the world and the world could've done nothing to make me feel good.

"I prefer to stand here on this glorious summer's day in this splendid country. That's the other reason I'm glad I came here. I discovered a country about which I had known very little. What I had heard was largely irrelevant, all about deserts and heat, snakes and deadly spiders. Nothing about bountiful and healthy food. Nothing about the beautiful countryside along the seashore, up to our astonishing Blue Mountains, and out to the green hills back here. Nothing about a government that keeps decent order without restricting the creative spirit and the drive of the people to fashion a prosperous life for themselves. Nothing about the open spirit of the community and of the optimism among its people. I am very happy to have found all this and I am thankful to be here."

Bernhardt paused and let his gaze wander over the audience.

"Excuse me for getting carried away," he smiled. "This is not what I really had planned to say, but the introduction made me think back to how I had started out here and how I feel about it now.

"We are gathered here to lay the foundation bricks for a real hospital. We have always had a tent hospital. I know it well. I spent six long months in it. It was freezing in winter, but I received proper treatment and I was able to walk out of it again, contrary to the expectations of most who saw me in there at first. I am grateful and now that I have the means I am happy to repay my debt with some extra interest. However, my donation is more than a thank you to the hospital, it is my farewell gift to the town of Hill End. I wanted to leave behind something of permanent use and of lasting service. Regardless of how the fortunes of gold will rise and fall, the solid building we have planned will remain to tell of our presence here in the 1860s and 1870s."

Subconsciously Bernhardt savoured the beauty of the tall trees around them, the sunlight playing in the leaves, the tranquility of the woods, the well dressed group of people before him.

"No, I'm not going back to Europe, nor to America, the awakening giant, as well I could. I am not taking the fortunes this country has bestowed on me to the mother country England as my colleague Edwards is doing. I am going to Sydney. My wife Harriet is already there with our little daughter, preparing for the birth of our new baby. But as I leave here I make the pledge that I will use my wealth to the utmost benefit of Australia. This country has been very generous to me. I will try to do the same. Where appropriate, I will be charitable, but I won't squander my hard-earned money."

Bernhardt glanced at Louis, who was known for his boundless generosity. "Rather, I intend to start new business ventures and trading relationships which will foster economic progress all around us. And above all, I will promote the image of Australia overseas. There is so much good news and exciting information to be disseminated about this country. We need more immigrants to fill the vacant spaces, to expand our economy, to develop the riches this continent has to offer. We will create good will towards Australia, towards its people, towards its traders and businessmen, even towards its scholars and artists."

"Hear, hear," sounded the approval from the audience.

"Nowadays we are only a colony of Great Britain. But one day, our great grandchildren will live in an independent nation. Britain has gone out into the world, like a man in his prime sowing his oats, indiscriminately fathering colonies as if siring children. The brood will grow up. They might come home to visit their parents, from exotic places like India and Africa, and one day they could create discomfort in the stale island home of England.

"Australia is an entire huge continent. It has the minerals, the farmland, the climate, and above all the right spirit to grow up to be a great and contented country. The fine hospital we are going to build here at Hill End will be one additional piece in the growing mosaic of our progressive and humane lifestyle. Last year we built the new public school here in solid red brick. We also have a few private schools in our community. Now and here, in these spacious grounds overlooking the town, we are laying the foundation for a gracious, solid and functional hospital. All exterior and interior walls will be constructed with our local brick. The design calls for some twenty windows with elegant round arches. A ten foot wide paved veranda will surround the entire building. Patients can be brought out there into sun or shade to breath invigorating oxygen that flows from the gum trees in the hills around us."

Finally, Bernhardt concluded by opening his arms in a wide gesture.

"This is one of the legacies I am proud to leave behind, in addition to a thriving mine and other businesses, a place for the benefit of fellow citizens from all walks of life in need of care. Let me finish by quoting a poem that befits the occasion.

> *There is a destiny that calls us brothers.*
> *No man lives unto himself alone.*
> *What we put into the life of others*
> *comes back into our own."*

Bernhardt stood on the platform in the clearing in the woods and bowed to the generous applause. He was surprised how well the speech had come off. Thirteen years ago he had hardly spoken any English. His wording may not have been perfect, but he didn't worry about little details nor about his accent. There were more important things that counted, to have a message worth telling and to have prepared all his thoughts in an orderly fashion, but above all to have the self-confidence to stand up and speak freely. Bernhardt felt he had this confidence now. He had persisted and beaten the odds in his life. He felt equal to the best of men, not superior, but certainly not inferior either. He was convinced he could tackle anything. As he stepped from the platform, Bernhardt smiled about his life, the past, the future he envisaged, but particularly about the way he felt at this moment.

Harriet had rented a large extravagant house in Sydney where the family lived awaiting construction of their home. In Bernhardt's absence she began to assemble the small army of servants they required to run the current house and particularly the new one to come. She selected a butler with a well-established reputation and she found an experienced housekeeper. They in turn hired the appropriate staff reporting to them. As a mark of respect the butler was addressed by the whole household as Mr Hogan, and the housekeeper as Mrs Packer even though she was not married. The butler retained two footmen. It was their duty to carry wood and coal for cooking and for fireplaces in winter, to trim the many oil and gas lamps, clean silverware, and most conspicuously, to announce visitors to the house. At such occasions the footmen had to look their best in imposing livery, showing off their well formed calves in silk stockings. Another opportunity for the footmen to impress outsiders was serving at dinner parties. On outings during the day a footman, in addition to the coachman, attended the mistress when she visited the couturier or went calling on friends. However, the Holtermanns did not adopt the custom prevailing in Britain to have two footmen riding on the back of the carriage in full uniform of coat, knee breeches and powdered hair when the family was driven to formal functions.

On their way to a ball or to the theatre, Mr Holtermann would be in formal eveningwear and Mrs Holtermann would dress elaborately in captivating colours. The venue might be the Royal Victoria Theatre in Sydney, or the Theatre Royal, or the Sydney Philharmonic Society. Once a year the fund-raising ball for St. Vincent's hospital was held at the lavishly decorated Exhibition Building in the presence of his Excellency the Governor and Lady Robinson, the Attorney General, members of parliament, university professors, representatives of the consular corps, distinguished military officers, and wealthy merchants and industrialists like the Holtermanns. Or Mr Holtermann would attend a business men's banquet at the Exchange, characterised by the huge sign covering a whole wall of the festive hall, reading, *'PEACE, GOODWILL, COMMERCE AMONG NATIONS'*.

The dutiful and patiently waiting coachman driving them on such occasions had also been hired by the butler. In addition, Mr Hogan had employed a groom and a gardener. The housekeeper, Mrs Packer, had found suitable housemaids. They cleaned the many rooms and hallways all day long, carried water to the bedrooms for washing and bathing and kept fires going when there was a chill in the air on winter mornings and evenings. In the big kitchen the maids helped the cook prepare sumptuous meals and the scullery maids washed vast quantities of dishes, pots and pans from morning till late in the evening besides doing the laundry for the family and the servants. Harriet had participated in the selection of her lady's maid and of the young nursemaid.

Bernhardt had arrived just in time to appoint the governess, Victoria. She would teach the children until they were old enough to go to school or college. Bernhardt was impressed by Victoria's competence. Despite her young age she was qualified to teach mathematics, history, natural sciences, German and French, music, dancing, and the use of celestial and terrestrial globes to convey heavenly and earthbound geography. The young governess had the deportment of a lady, befitting her position, which put her a cut above the level of the other higher ranking servants, Mrs Packer and Mr Hogan. What struck Mr Holtermann when he was talking to her was not so much her tall and handsome appearance, but the joyful emotion her presence released in him.

They were still at the rented mansion when Bernhardt and Harriet celebrated in grand style the christening of their second daughter, Harriet Esther. During the garden party, Bernhardt talked with the architect he had chosen to build his residence.

"The news is not so good," the architect was saying. "Perhaps we should not talk about it today. These festivities are too elegant to be spoilt by anything."

"Do tell me, I'm not upset easily. Where are we standing with the project?"

"Well, it appears to be certain now that we won't get Balls Head. The council wants to keep the peninsula as a public reserve. It will not be sold to anybody, not even to you, regrettably, Mr Holtermann."

Bernhardt shook his head and smiled. "These stubborn mongrels. Of course, I haven't had much time to make myself familiar to them. All they know about me are the newspaper reports from the goldfields. And the journalists are not exactly in love with me, these begrudging idealists. They would only be happy if I gave everybody and his brother a share of my wealth. But would they be willing to work eight years in the dirt, in the cold wet darkness of a mineshaft? Would they risk everything they have? Would they starve and beg to keep a business going?"

The architect agreed. "Of course not, that's why they are socialists. They would prefer to get a free share of what others have toiled for. They are even planning to set up their own political party, and they are talking about income tax on business. Imagine that. They probably want to choke commerce right out of existence. Who would pay the salaries then? Who would buy the advertising that pays their wages?"

Bernhardt took a drink before he replied. "Luckily, there are a few, even at the newspapers, who see the bigger picture, who recognise the benefit of business and of international commerce to the wider community, who understand the longterm detriment caused by restrictions and overtaxation. But back to our building plans. Balls Head in the harbour is out then. I would have enjoyed the commanding view it has of Sydney."

"Apparently, the councillors also didn't like the possibility that you might have turned the peninsula into an island."

"Well, it was a worthwhile consideration. It would have greatly increased the security of the whole family. I could have enemies, you know. A bridge would have controlled security nicely. But, we must accept the decision. Our second choice is not so bad either."

"Indeed. The eight acre site available on St Leonards Hill above Lavender Bay is easier to reach. The view across the bay to the centre of Sydney is better, too. This will be excellent for your photographic projects."

"Yes, that's very important. We'll have clear sight of the tall ships, reaching from Sydney Cove across Walsh Bay to Darling Harbour. Beyond that we'll get the view over the whole city as far as Botany Bay. And in the west the Blue

Mountains will form the horizon." Bernhardt was excited. "To capture all this properly in photographs, it would be best to have a tower. It should be a hundred feet high," he estimated. "From its flat top I can capture a complete panorama in a continuous series of pictures. For the exhibition we could assemble a picture of Sydney twenty feet wide."

"Let's see," the architect calculated. "The ceilings are fourteen feet high, two storeys, plus the roof. Yes, we can do that, a tower, more or less in the centre of the building. Around the front section we'll have the two storey veranda with the stone balcony set back above." The architect grinned, "After talking to your wife, I am up to twenty principal rooms now, with additional supporting quarters and servants' lodgings."

"That's right. We'll build what we need, not a room less. There are already quite a few impressive sandstone houses in North Sydney. We don't want to devalue the neighbourhood."

They laughed. "It is a beautiful site," glowed the architect while a footman refilled their glasses. "With the grassy hill rolling down towards Lavender Bay, marked by shrubs and trees. You'll have Sir Thomas Dibbs as neighbour with his massive stone residence Graythwaite, and John Carr's two storey mansion in beautiful gardens with a natural waterfall. Further up lives George Lavender and his wife Susannah. And just down the road is the quaint sandstone Church of St Peter."

"Yes, its not just dairy farms and orchards any more."

"The school is under construction, too, and we have some industry developing on the wider North Shore, like James King's glass making company in Mosman and Albert Radke's tannery in Lane Cove."

"All we need now, is a bridge across the harbour," said Mr Holtermann, broaching one of his favourite subjects, "to connect us to Sydney. I have to get into Parliament to be able to push the idea. When the time comes I will even offer a substantial contribution towards the financing of a bridge. This is a community project well worth supporting."

"James Milson's steam ferries are not too bad, though. He has four now, each carrying sixty passengers. But there are not enough punts to transfer carriages and wagons."

"Yes, a bridge is inevitable. It could even bring a train line across to go north," Bernhardt reasoned.

"That would be asking too much of the punts."

They chuckled.

"And since you mentioned money, Mr Holtermann, we would need some funds at the ready to make a bid for the land and to make progress payments to builders when we start construction."

"Yes, that's well in hand. Give me accounts."

Bernhardt thought that his mining shares were close to peak value now and he was planning to sell. He knew it was a tradeoff between greed and fear. Soon the shares would fall. No investor had ever lost money by getting out early. Other funds were coming in from the businesses he was selling at Hill End.

"As long as you don't mix your mortar with salt water," Bernhardt joked while making his way towards the other guests. "Like Mr Levy did at Cammeray, and the house collapsed."

"Not only that, he repeated the process and the same thing happened again." They laughed jovially.

"Not surprisingly people now call his little peninsula 'Folly Point'."

The host excused himself from the architect. "I'll mingle with my guests and future neighbours. Perhaps I can learn from them about projects to finance in Sydney. And as we discussed earlier, if you come across any good real estate investment opportunities, let me know."

The following week Bernhardt saw his stockbroker and instructed him to sell off his mining stocks gradually, quietly, and without disclosing who the vendor was. As he left the building, he met Hunt.

"Fancy that, meeting one of the Hill End workers here in Sydney," Bernhardt said jovially. "I thought I had left that life."

"Yes, you are getting too fancy for us now," replied Hunt with a thin smile that left it open as to whether he was joking or not. "I read you are now one of the wealthiest men in Australia. Did you just buy some more shares in there? Everybody is excited about our mines now. I'm seeing a broker, too. I've waited long enough. But now I'll invest all my savings in goldmining stocks."

"Well, it could still go on for a while. But we are perhaps at the peak now. You know the gold claims out there. What is your estimate as to when they'll run out of gold? The gold yield is in decline. No new veins are being discovered."

"Are you trying to discourage me? This is typical of you capitalists. You want to keep it all to yourselves. You want to keep people like me out. That's how I've always known you. You think you are smarter, like the time when you insisted on driving the shaft deeper instead of going sideways. Then suddenly we saw these photographs in all the newspapers of you and our big nugget."

"You are jumping from one subject to another, Hunt. All I was saying was that gold investment will slow down soon. I'm just trying to be helpful. My advice would be not to stay in goldmining stocks for too long."

"There you have it. That's the opposite of what Louis Beyers told me. He said he'd never sell his shares. He'll keep them for life. And he's almost as rich as you are. He's not leaving Hill End either, as some people are. He's doing a fine job as our mayor. Louis is the most generous person I know; he gives to everybody and to every cause. Not a typical capitalist at all."

"I am glad to hear about Louis. If you're going back, give him my regards, and to Mary as well. Tell them Harriet and I think of them often. They don't reply to the letters we write. They must be busy. I wish them all the best."

Bernhardt went to his club across the street. He looked the gentleman he had become, wearing a pristine frock coat, elegant boots, a top hat and gloves, carrying an expensive watch chain and a debonair cane. In the club he ran into Mark Hammond. Mark and his family had moved to Sydney where they had bought a large house in Paddington. In the course of their conversation Bernhardt learnt that Mark had sold all his goldmining stocks. They talked about Edwards who had already sold the year before and who had now returned to England.

Glancing across the newspapers, Bernhardt's attention was caught by a report about the visit by the Governor to Hill End. His Excellency Sir Hercules Robinson had been welcomed with a triumph of decorous enthusiasm, it said. His speech at the grand banquet was printed in full. It started with comments on the rough coach journey from Bathurst, which had left him feeling as if he had been passed through one of Hill End's quartz crushing machines. The Governor's address continued:

> Ever since my arrival in New South Wales I have heard of the marvellous wealth of your golden mountain, and have felt a strong desire to inspect the place for myself; but I may say that the picture which my fancy had painted fell far short of the reality which I have witnessed since my arrival here. I had seen a photograph taken about eighteen months ago, with a bullock team drawing a wagon out of a swamp opposite the door of this hotel. I had heard, also, that a couple of years ago the place consisted only of a few hovels; and judging too, by the approach, I certainly did not expect to find much of a settlement at the end of it. But to my surprise I found a

large, well laid out town, with straight streets, and well built stores and business premises, four churches and parsonages, three banks, two newspapers, a public school, and a hospital, and, in short, an appearance on all sides of comfort and stability and importance which would have been creditable in a city of fifty years standing.

Bernhardt was pleased to hear the hospital mentioned, and well built stores, some of which he had had constructed.

As regards the population, I thought that perhaps I might have been met by a few hundred of rough but enthusiastic miners; but, to my astonishment, I was received at the entrance to the town by about three thousand well dressed, orderly, and intelligent men and women, accompanied by about five hundred of as beautiful children as ever I saw in my life, and the whole procession headed by the members of the various societies of Oddfellows, Freemasons and Temperance Unions, whilst the whole body appeared to me to be animated by a feeling of enthusiastic loyalty, which convinced me that, although oceans separate you from the old country, your hearts are British still, and that you retain in your distant isolated mountain home of Tambaroora those feelings of personal devotion to the Queen, respect for constituted authority, and love of law and order, which form the marked characteristics of the Anglo Saxon race. I must say I think it is too much the fashion in New South Wales to depreciate mining communities, and to compare them unfavourably in consequence of their roving, unsettled and speculative character with those who are engaged in pastoral and agricultural pursuits. I think it is unjust. If it were not for these special characteristics, the miners would all probably be shepherds or husband men, and whatever question there may be as to whether such pursuits would or would not be more to their own advantage, there can be no doubt whatever that, without the aid of the mining community, the colony would never have advanced with the unexampled rapidity which it has done in commerce, in industry, and in wealth. I should like to know how many hundreds of years must have elapsed before Australia would have attained to its present prosperity if it had been dependent alone for its progression upon wool and wheat, tallow and hides. But the gold discovery and the energy of the miners had developed Tambarooras and Gulgongs, and Bendigos and Ballarats, over the whole country.

In reading the Governor's speech, Bernhardt felt proud to have been one of the principal protagonists in the speedy development of Australia.

Cities have been raised in the primeval forests, and the homes of civilisation have been reared in places where a few years since there was only the wigwam of the savage. Having had an opportunity of inspecting today most of your principal mines, I must say that it gave me great pleasure to find that they were all being worked in an honest, open, and straightforward manner in the interest of their shareholders, and not with any reference to the manoeuvres of the bulls and the bears of the Sydney Stock Exchange. I was much amused a few weeks since in Sydney to hear one morning that the city was much depressed as Krohmann's had only declared a dividend of 12s. 6d. Now, considering that this dividend was 62 per cent upon the original capital, and considering also that the mine had yielded a few months before 20s. 6d., making a total cash return in about nine months of 165 per cent on capital, I confess I could not see any great cause for depression. Solomon has wisely said that there are three things that are never satisfied, yea, four things say not 'it is enough'. The grave; and the barren womb; the earth that is not filled with water; and the fire that saith not, it is enough.' I think that if

Solomon had lived in our day, he might have added to his list the stock jobbers of the Sydney Exchange.

Gentlemen, I will not detain you longer, but will merely once more ask you to believe that I shall never, as long as I live, forget the gratifying reception you gave to me yesterday, and ever feel the deepest interest and sympathy in your welfare and prosperity. Allow me to propose: Success to Hill End and the mining interests of the district.

1874

MIRACULOUS PHOTOGRAPHS

Beaufoy Merlin and his assistant, Charles Bayliss, had come to Sydney with Bernhardt Holtermann to continue their photographic cooperation. Merlin did not live to see the completion of Holtermann's house. The strong and imposing looking artist succumbed to decades of working with photographic chemicals. At the age of forty-three he died, surrounded by his wife and children, at his house at Leichhardt. Bayliss continued his work.

The Holtermanns' grand residence in an English architectural style was nearing completion. Below the stone balustrade of a lofty roof-top terrace, two storied wings extended from the main building. The ground floor section of the veranda was under construction, with five high arches between graceful double columns. A second story veranda was to be built above it. Tall chimneys reached towards the sky. Rising above it all was the massive square tower in the centre, repeating at its flat top the ornamental balustrade of the stone balcony, accented by spires at each corner.

Gardeners were planting flower beds and shrubbery. Viewed from the bottom of the expansive hill reaching up from Lavender Bay, the mansion glistened in the sun like a crown.

In the elegantly completed library, Bernhardt was talking with Charles Bayliss.

"Our friend Beaufoy," Bernhardt recounted, "just before his death, wrote an interesting article in the *Town and Country Journal*. But to put it in context, let me read you this from the

Melbourne *Argus* about the end of the International Exhibition in Vienna."

He picked up the newspaper.

"It was a magnificent affair," Bernhardt read out, "set in 450 acres of park land beside the Danube, but our country was lamentably conspicuous by its absence. Where all the world is on show, not to be there is to argue yourself unknown."

Bernhardt took the journal.

"And this is part of what our Beaufoy wrote in his last article:

Why should we not display the country's resources in prominent places, show to the overcrowded nations of Europe what a fine field there is here for honest labour and the investment of capital? It pains one to note the listlessness with which people hear about an exhibition, in which various specimens of the country's mineral resources, of her unrivalled timber, of her infant industries will be brought together, and made clear to all who take the trouble of opening their eyes. On social, commercial, and political grounds it is the bounden duty of the people of this country to prove to the world that she has within her territory the material of future greatness; and it is to be hoped all men with true patriotic spirit will cooperate with Mr. Holtermann in demonstrating on a large scale the country's wealth, and its attractiveness as a scene of industrial operations. How much more telling will an exhibition be, when displayed in the United Kingdom and principal cities of Europe, than mere statistical statements, Agents-general letters, or the speeches of paid lecturers. I firmly believe that thousands will yet be attracted hither by the Holtermann display, who would not otherwise leave the old world, or if they did, would seek a new home in the United States of America.

Now, what do you say to that, Charles?"

"He was indeed a man of many talents, our dear Beaufoy.

He taught me all he knew about photography, but nothing about writing articles. He sure made his point clearly with this one."

"Talking about exhibits," Bernhardt continued the thought, "let's inspect one of the vantage points for our photographs. The staircase in the tower has just been finished. Let's go up."

"Oh, fantastic, I've been looking forward to that."

"The next World Exhibition will be in Philadelphia in 1876," Bernhardt explained on the way. "Two years sounds like a long time to get ready. But in fact, it could just be enough. We have to determine the specifications of the lenses we need to produce our giant pictures. Then we get the optics cut and assembled in Germany. Even the steamboats still take a long time to come from Europe. We must allow a year for the lenses to be here. Then we'll give it a try. Pictures of this size will be a world first, perhaps six feet wide. Since the negatives need to be the same size as the final prints, the glass plates will be enormous. If we succeed, we'll have just enough time for preparation of the exhibits and for shipment to Philadelphia."

"Photographs of such dimensions have never been produced. I don't think it is possible. When we hand-coat the glass plate to make a negative of such proportions, the collodion will be dry on one end before we are finished at the other, yet the exposure needs to take place while the negative is wet. I see other practical difficulties, how to get an even coating of silver nitrate this size, how to handle the weight of the huge glass, and how to prepare a fixing bath of dangerous potassium cyanide in these dimensions."

Bernhardt didn't answer. He had thought of these things too. But the photographic exhibition was another of his dreams. And he'd make good his dream, problems or not.

They reached the platform at the top of the tower.

"What a view," Charles exclaimed. He let his eyes sweep around in a circle. "What a panorama!"

"Yes, this is what we want to present overseas, the world's

most beautiful harbour, one of the most captivating sights created in collaboration between nature and man. But it will only be appreciated if the size of the image is impressive enough."

"I agree with that. But what camera will we use, and how would we get such a monster ever up here?"

"Ha, ha, Charles, my friend, it is impossible, isn't it? The answer is, no camera at all. We'll build a room up here as wide as the tower, and we'll put the lenses in the walls of the room. That will be our camera. We'll be inside the camera, preparing the negative, mounting it against the back wall. For the exposure we'll open the aperture from the inside. We'll try to produce pictures six feet wide and four feet high. And we'll join some of them together for a broad vista, as wide as twenty or thirty feet."

"Incredible. Nothing like it has ever been done anywhere. But this sight justifies our best efforts. We could use various lenses, wide angle and long. The detail will be astounding, probably better than what we see now with our bare eyes."

"Exactly. So, that's what we have to calculate, the measurements of the optics related to the space up here. Then we'll get the room built, vibration free and airtight. What an adventure, Charles, such an advance in the exciting new field of photography!"

"My hometown, Melbourne, has taller buildings than Sydney, picturesque avenues, too, vast city parks and gardens. Government House has a tower as well. If you want me to go, I could take a three hundred and sixty degree panorama from the tower. There are plenty of other subjects, all the impressive bank buildings and merchant houses, built of beautiful marble or granite."

"Of course you'll go, Charles. You've got the spirit. In the meantime I'll prepare other exhibits to present the unique environment of our continent to the world."

1876

FAREWELL FROM SYDNEY

Harriet was in the morning room, elegantly clothed in a bustle –a dress with a large hump at the lower back, a style which had developed from the voluminous crinoline. The crinoline had been a wide skirt support made of linen or horsehair or even built as a frame construction. These inflated skirts had made it difficult to walk through narrow doorways and could be very embarrassing if caught by a strong wind. To sit down in it had been no joy, and it also used to sweep bricabrac off parlour tables. Now the design had been sensibly cut back in front and on the sides.

Harriet was talking to her children's governess, Victoria, who was wearing a print dress. Victoria was young and attractive, which had initially made Harriet uneasy about employing her. However, there was one aspect of Victoria's appearance which made her less appealing in Harriet's opinion, a slight obliquity of vision. Even after so many years of marriage to Bernhardt, Harriet did not know that this was a feature he found most enchanting.

"Oh, Victoria, I'm so excited about our trip. Only a few more days and we'll board our steamer, the *City of San Francisco*."

"How fitting! The ship has the same name as our destination."

"Yes, our first stop. But there will be many others. We'll really see the world. Two years, Mr Holtermann is saying. It'll be quite an experience for Sophia and Esther. Imagine, at their age I'd never been outside Bathurst." She shook her head, letting her mind drift back for a moment. "Victoria, it'll be good to have you along, to look after the children and to continue with their instruction."

Bernhardt had made it clear to Harriet that in addition to the two children they could only take one servant on the long journey. The army of domestics which ran Holtermann Hall had to stay behind.

"It will be more than just a governess' job for you," Harriet continued. "You'll be my lady's maid as well as looking after the girls without their nursemaid."

Victoria thought it would be a welcome change from her current position in the household, where she was a bit distant from the other servants, and of course from the adult family members as well. "What an opportunity to be taken on such an exciting journey," she exclaimed. "Do you think I may be able to see some of the international exhibition in Philadelphia?"

"Yes, Victoria. Although it'll be about the time that the baby's due. It's bad timing, but I wouldn't miss the trip for anything. And Mr Holtermann will be pleased to see the baby immediately, not a year or two later."

"I hope it won't be too strenuous for you, Madam."

Harriet was not worried about that. They were booked in first class accommodation on the ship, trains, and hotel suites, the *crème de la crème*, with plenty of additional local servants to attend them everywhere. The trip wasn't going to be taxing.

Victoria considered Mrs Holtermann's tenacity and thought out aloud. "You've been extremely busy ever since my arrival, getting the new household set up, the furnishings, the staff, and then the great dinner parties you organised with such success."

Harriet nodded and smiled. The dinners had been her major effort in making their way into the local society, as Bernhardt made more and more acquaintances during business interactions, at the club and at the Masonic Lodge where he was a member. Harriet studied the etiquette books carefully. And when they were invited, she paid attention to all details of hospitality provided.

The guests the Holtermanns invited usually accepted gladly, impressed by the new mansion, and curious about its interior and its owners. Bernhardt and Harriet decided on the proper selection of company for each occasion to match people who were socially comfortable together. To foster easy conversation and to establish closer liaison with their visitors they normally invited no more than ten guests to a dinner. The footmen in their elegant uniforms would show arrivals into the drawing room for an initial chitchat. Before the formal promenade in to dinner, Harriet and Bernhardt would circulate discreetly to mix up the couples, making sure the appropriate gentlemen were paired off with ladies of befitting status. The assembly looked impressive in their prescribed attire, gentlemen in black trousers, waistcoat and long jacket, with white tie, shirt and gloves, the ladies in formal long evening dresses of rich fabrics, with frills and adornments of mainly bluish hues, enhanced by jewellery and feathers, very expressive outfits, which looked less bold in the soft yellowish light of the gas lamps and candles. When the butler announced that dinner was served and the couples proceeded into the dining room, they were impressed by the opulent furnishings and by the table setting, from the great heavy many-armed candlestick holder, fashionably called the *epergne*, resting on a silver platform at the centre of the table on damasked cloth, to the heavy silver plate and crystal. Guests were pleased with the attentive butler and his silent, efficient footmen.

Dinner would traditionally run to ten courses, not counting dessert, coffee and walnuts. Harriet had thought of everything, including the bill of fare placed next to every person. She would select dishes which took advantage of the full abundance of local produce, from fresh oysters to fish, mussels, prawns, crayfish, Balmain bugs and yabbies, going on to lamb, beef, mutton and fowl, all served with the appropriate vegetables and salads. Two servants attended exclusively to the wine, from sherry and Madeira to the reds and whites. After the main courses the tablecloth would be removed and desserts would be served with champagne. Then the ladies would withdraw to the drawing room for coffee or tea, while the gentlemen circulated the port. Mr Holtermann would have an opportunity to touch on some business matters while others might indulge in some risqué story telling. When Bernhardt perceived some guests were getting too free in their speech he would suggest that it was time to join the ladies. There was another hour of mixed conversation in the drawing room before the carriages were called, except for those occasions when the dinner was followed by a dance.

"Yes, I'll miss our dinner parties and the friends we've made," Harriet reflected. "We were truly busy with all return invitations and with the ladies who began calling on me during the day, as we became known in Sydney society."

"Your last dinner invitation was at Northbridge," Victoria recalled. "At Mr Arthur Twemlow's house, The Hermitage, you told me."

"The house is two stories in sandstone," Mrs Holtermann recalled, "surrounded by beautiful gardens, with a huge fig tree in the centre. He quarried the stone for the building on his own estate along Middle Harbour."

"Middle Harbour, that's where his footman drowned, isn't it?"

"Yes, what a drama. It's not practical to live so far out if you have a business in Sydney. The footman has to take Twemlow by boat through The Spit and around Middle Head to the Quay, from where he walks to his jewellery shop in Sydney Arcade. On the journey home the sailing boat got caught in a violent storm and the servant drowned. Twemlow was fortunate to escape."

Mrs Holtermann got up and walked to the window, looking through the park across the harbour to the city.

"The Holts also used to live far away, all the way south at Botany Bay," Victoria commented on other friends of the family.

"What a grand home," Mrs Holtermann recalled vividly, "called Sans Souci."

"I heard Thomas Holt built it for his German wife who named it after the palace of the Prussian King Frederick the Great, Sans Souci." They laughed.

"It used to take a while to get there," Mrs Holtermann remembered. "It's so far south of the city."

To go there for the evening she and her maid had to start laying out her dress, the elaborate underwear and all fancy accessories in the morning, to be ready to start dressing right after lunch. The butler would send a servant down to the point to let Milson's men know when the vehicular ferry would be required and to reserve it for the Holtermann's carriage. The ferry man would also be told to stand by well after midnight to bring them back across the harbour. By mid afternoon, with the horses groomed and readied, the carriage would be waiting as Mrs Holtermann emerged, dressed from shoes to hat in voluptuous, colourful finery. After the carriage had crossed the harbour on the steam punt, they would pick up Mr Holtermann at his office in the city, to start the journey to Sans Souci, which would take them the best part of two hours.

"Small wonder Mrs Holt found the location too isolated," Mrs Holtermann commented. "She didn't want to live down there, even in the most beautiful mansion. So her husband built her another house at Marrickville overlooking Cook's River. It's that easy if you have enough money," Mrs Holtermann smiled. "My husband likes these people, because she is German, I imagine. And he goes hunting with Mr Holt."

"Is it true that he breeds rabbits for hunting? And that he keeps exotic animals, like alpaca?"

"Yes, as exotic as their entertainment, which is lavish indeed." Mrs Holtermann sat down by the window. "There is another German friend of Mr Holtermann's not far from here at Lane Cove, Albert Radke. He has his leather belt factory there."

"Leather belts run all the modern machinery nowadays, driven by steam engines," Victoria commented. "That would be a good business to be in."

"Another place that invites us regularly on our side of the harbour is Dallwood Home, the mansion of Theodore Gurney at Seaforth." Mrs Holtermann smiled, wagging her head slightly at the thought of its owner. "What a smart and entertaining character he is, our professor of mathematics and natural philosophy. He is well off, so he doesn't have to bother writing learned papers for publication to further his reputation."

"You truly had a busy social calendar," Victoria nodded. "And now the last few weeks have been even more hectic, preparing for the voyage."

"Yes, I've had my hands full these past years, but it was a rewarding experience to explore the ins and outs of refined society. It feels good to take charge and give a sense of direction to your household. It's a serious feat, but it's not like struggling for survival. I don't wake up in the middle of the night any more, worrying whether we will eat tomorrow. I worried about that often, you know, in the early days at Hill End."

It was hard to imagine, Victoria thought, looking at all the luxury that surrounded them. Going out on a limb with incredible persistence and hard work, that's where the wealth came from, she reasoned.

"Yes, you and Mr Holtermann have been so occupied," Victoria repeated. "Mr Holtermann had to finalise his exhibits and ship everything off to America."

The exhibition was part of the official New South Wales

Government stand. Mr Holtermann was now preparing his personal presentation to take on board. Mounted on a canvas it was eighty feet wide and five feet high. This was to be unrolled and shown when he gave talks, displaying the giant photographs. He had planned presentations to be made in England, Germany, France, Switzerland, and even India.

Bill Slack was appointed as manager to look after all Holtermann businesses while the family was absent. The Holtermanns had known him since he had run a hotel at Hill End, a competitor to their own hotel. He was also postmaster. Everybody was leaving Hill End. The gold had run out. There were only a few farms there now. Houses wouldn't sell and people just packed up and left. Chan, the grocer and old friend of the Holtermanns came to Sydney with their help and was given one of Bernhardt's stores in Dixon Street rent free for a time, to get started.

Harriet picked up the *Sydney Evening News*. "It says here they found Dr. Livingstone in Africa after all these years. The *New York Herald* sent an explorer to track him down." After perusing the paper for a while, she continued, "Victoria, would you please read me this article Mr Holtermann has pointed out to me. He mentioned it's about our trip. I'll sit by the window here and enjoy the view as long as we are still here to savour it."

Victoria took the newspaper and began to read aloud.

"Mr. B. O. Holtermann, the well known goldminer, and one of the richest men in the colony, claims to have produced the largest photographic views in the world. This is, of course, saying a great deal. Our Yankee friends who are proverbial for big things, may possibly be inclined to dispute Australia's claims to photographic superiority. Apart from the size of the pictures, they are splendid specimens of the photographer's art, the outlines being sharp and clear, and the various objects shown coming out prominently before the eye. The difficulty of producing pictures of such size can best be understood and appreciated by photographers, among many of whom, we understand, it is believed that it is not possible to execute photographs of such magnitude. If such a belief exists, Mr Holtermann claims to have dispelled it, and to have worked a revolution in the art of photography. The whole of the perspective is shown much clearer than can be seen with the naked eye. Signboards between two and three miles off can be seen easily. These views are the principal ones; but Mr Holtermann's studio is stocked with thousands of photographic views, all splendid works of art, of different parts of New South Wales and Victoria. It is his intention to start for England next year with his grand panorama, his principal object being to induce immigrants to come to Australia."

Victoria put the newspaper down.

"Well, the reporter got most of it right," commented Harriet. "Which is unusual for a newspaper man. He left out the World Fair in America completely and jumped directly to England, without mentioning the rest of Europe on our itinerary. The writer must be British, but at least he has a good attitude, not as destructive as many journalists. They call it being critical and that means being condemnatory. That report was well above the norm. Thank you, Victoria. You read beautifully. What a clever girl you are. We'll have a good time together on this journey."

1876

AMERICA

It was on a memorable occasion that Victoria read to Harriet again from the newspaper. They had settled in a good hotel in the town of Burlington, in the State of Iowa, two hundred miles from Chicago. Harriet was resting and beside her lay sleeping her one day old son. The pregnancy had been a familiar routine for Harriet this time, even during the extensive journey. She enjoyed being admired and pampered. And she had taken the delivery in her stride. The baby was strong and healthy. Life was beautiful, Harriet thought. Bernhardt was extremely pleased and proud about the new addition to his growing family. He only missed having friends and associates around with whom to share the joyous occasion.

Late in the afternoon Harriet and Victoria were alone with the infant in the hotel suite.

"The newspaper is called *Burlington Hawk Eye*," Victoria proclaimed. "Here is what they say about the Holtermanns:

There was a native Australian born in Burlington yesterday. B. O. Holtermann, a resident of Sydney, Australia, and a member of an extensive firm, Holtermann & Company, of that place, is on his way with his wife and daughters and a servant to Hamburg, Germany. Careful of the comfort of his family, he chose the shortest and safest route across the continent, which is well known to be the C.B.&Q. (Chicago, Burlington and Quincy Railroad) and Holtermann, after changing the through checks for his baggage for depot checks, sought and obtained commodious and comfortable quarters at the Barrett House, where, in Room Number 39, within two hours, a son was born unto him whom he would do well to christen 'Burlington'."

"Doesn't sound too bad, actually, Burlington," Mrs Holtermann mused. "It certainly would remind us of the special circumstances. That way we can take the birthplace with us, since probably none of us will ever see this town again. But you said Bernie got another newspaper for us to read?"

"Yes, this one is from San Francisco. That's going back a while. It mentions Mr Holtermann's presentation there. Here it is:

"The Photographic Society of the Pacific Coast held a regular monthly meeting last evening in the galleries of Messrs Bradley & Ralston, Montgomery Street, San Francisco. Mr Ralston proposed the name of B. O. Holtermann, of Australia, for membership. Mr Ralston offered the following resolution: That as photographers we are indebted to the liberality of B. O. Holtermann for demonstrating the possibility and perfecting the production of the largest negative, and we tender him the thanks of this Society for kindly placing the negative on view for inspection. Mr Holtermann begged the Society to accept his sincere thanks for the reception he had received in San Francisco by the fellow members of his profession."

Bernhardt entered the hotel room. He kissed Harriet and took the baby into his arms.

"How is our little Burlington?" he asked playfully. "Our American-Australian-German. And where are the girls?"

"They were invited to play with the hotelier's children," explained Harriet. "It helps that we are all speaking the same language."

"How do you feel now, my dear?"

"Surprisingly well. In a few days we should be able to travel to Philadelphia. We don't want the Great Exhibition to wait for us for too long."

"There's no rush at all. The show's on for quite a while. We're not missing much, a function or a reception perhaps, but there'll be more. The only event we should be there for is the closing ceremony, in case we receive a prize for our contribution. The main thing is that you and the baby are healthy. I'm so happy, another boy at last!"

He placed the baby carefully down beside Harriet. "I'm hungry. Should we have meals sent up?"

"No thanks, not for me," smiled Harriet.

"On the other hand," Bernhardt considered, "I wouldn't mind going out to sample a nice local restaurant."

"Yes, why don't you do that, see some of the town? I'll be all right. And take Victoria with you. She hasn't been out since we arrived here. I'll sleep for a while."

"Are you sure?" Bernhardt hesitated before nodding his head. "I'll tell them downstairs to ask for the midwife to pay you a visit again. For the rest of the time they should have a maid look in on you regularly." He kissed Harriet and turned to the governess. "Victoria, would you like to join me in exploring a typical American town, chosen at random?"

"For study and research purposes. I would be delighted, Sir."

The hotel obligingly followed Mr Holtermann's requests and upon his inquiry also recommended a restaurant. Bernhardt and Victoria took a carriage on that brilliant summer evening.

In the elegant restaurant the windows were wide open. They made their selection from the menu and Bernhardt chose a light French wine. Initially in their conversation, Bernhardt's mind was on the exhibition.

"The Philadelphia Centennial is extremely popular. I was told that the best attendance so far for one day was more than a quarter of a million visitors. As it runs for 159 days, perhaps ten million spectators will see our great Australian pictures. That will really put our magnificent country on the map."

"And you, too, Mr Holtermann. You will be one of the accomplished and famous men of our day and age. I feel very honoured to be escorted by such a gentleman today."

"The pleasure is all mine, to have the company of such a beautiful and clever lady."

During the sumptuous meal Bernhardt's tone of voice and what he had to say soon became unusually personal. He smiled faintly. "I have been a secret admirer of yours ever since your interview and I was thrilled when Harriet decided to bring you on this trip. To have you near tingles all my senses."

Victoria looked straight at him, which didn't appear all that straight to Bernhardt, the slight turn in her eye arousing him strangely. She responded slowly. "I appreciate your candour, but as the situation is, we can't allow our feelings to come into play. I don't deny that we might both sense attractions, each for different reasons. But our roles in life are too different. I respect you deeply, I respect your wife and the whole life you have built for yourselves. I must be grateful for whatever small part I am allowed to play in it. Any other thought on my part would be impertinent."

"You may not know it, but you're making things worse, Victoria. Had you indicated you resented me I would've had to accept that. But from what you say I see a light glowing behind the barriers and conventions that separate us. If you know anything about me you'd know that nothing makes my will stronger than glimmering gold that is difficult to obtain."

Victoria was becoming distressed. "I honestly don't know what to do since any word I say will make matters worse. In the past I couldn't escape noticing how you'd touch my arm in conversation once in while when we were not observed, and I felt the force of a constellation that was waiting to overpower us both."

"In the bustling household I tried to be restrained and discreet, and your behaviour was always polite and correct, not revealing any emotions."

"Thank you," she nodded. "I'm acting this way to keep my job, Sir. To behave in any other way I'd be out on the street as soon as Mrs Holtermann became suspicious. If we were closer I'd lose your companionship completely." She looked straight at him once more. "So, whatever admiration I feel for a great man like you, I contain and control my emotions for my sake and yours."

Bernhardt shook his head. "I had no idea you'd given me so much as a thought. I had noticed nothing. Young ladies are supposed to be emotional and impulsive, aren't they?"

"Yes, we play that part when it is expected of us. It's one of our masks for fun and games, a way to achieve our ends in the short term. But I try to take a longer view and I certainly wouldn't play games with you. I have too much respect for you and for Mrs Holtermann. Your life is well balanced and I wouldn't want to be the one to disturb that balance, even if I were able. It'd be too destructive."

As the meal progressed, accentuated by the smooth wine shimmering in their glasses, Bernhardt became perplexed.

"You confound me with your sensitivity and intellect. You're pretending to put me on a pedestal, to hold me at a safe distance, to keep me motionless and emotionless like a statue."

Victoria laughed, revealing her splendid teeth. "I told you, I'm neither pretending, nor playing any game. Your life is an example to many."

The waiter refilled their glasses while the pair looked quietly at each other until Bernhardt interrupted their thoughts. "You made me think of something I never talk about." He pulled a leather wallet from his coat pocket and took out a small piece of paper. "I have written down my goals and I look at them regularly. Writing my aspirations down clarifies them, forcing me to think about my ultimate intentions."

Victoria felt drawn closer to Bernhardt. She was keen to see a new side of the man she admired, to find out more about his thoughts and emotions. "Now that you've told me, may I take a look at the list?" she asked.

"It could be hard for you to make out in this light, but I can read a few lines to you if you don't laugh," he conceded.

"It starts out, General Purposes: To leave the world a better place than I found it. To make a positive difference in the lives of others. Main Vehicle: Become an educator. Aims: Influence people to take responsibility for their own life, their own destiny. Persuade them to change the traditional road map that was handed down to them, to break with past legacies, to discard old superstitions, to escape restricting governments, oppressive employers, pre-assigned roles. To urge enterprising, open-minded men and women out of their European confinement. Induce them to draw their own road map in Australia. Sway them to break the fixed life pattern that holds them down in the old world to start a more diverse and prosperous life at sunnier shores for themselves and their descendants. You are smiling, Victoria."

"Yes, it is the smile of recognition. So that is what the eighty foot canvas is all about. This is the essence of the presentation that goes with it, the purpose behind it all. But excuse me for having interrupted you. I can see how useful it is to have a clearly defined mission in life. It sets out your priorities. Are there any other goals on your list?"

"There are more." He put the note away while he was talking. "I've changed over the years. I used to be more selfish. Now I am looking for opportunities to give and to help, but I might still be too judgmental about it. On the other hand, if I look at my friend Louis Beyers, he gives freely to anybody who asks. I heard, as mayor of Hill End he was paying the town's expenses from his own pocket. Some of his initiatives may well have lasting value, like the hundreds of trees he imported from Germany and had planted to form a great avenue into Hill End. But he helped the deserving and also the undeserving. Now he is running out of money and he cannot even assist the worthiest of causes any more."

"That's the point socialists seem to forget," Victoria commented. "There are limited resources, even for a government. Forcing a redistribution of wealth reduces business activity and dries up those resources. Help is warranted only when it assists a person's initiatives and leads to greater good than the support given. Free handouts perversely stop progress, for an individual and for society."

"Victoria, I cannot believe how smart you are! You know how to find clear words for the foggy ideas I sense at the centre of my convictions." He shook his head slowly and reflectively took up his glass.

"What other aims have you got recorded in your little note?" Victoria asked.

"Well, along the line of leaving Australia a better place than I found it, I would like to create new business and work opportunities. On this trip I'll speak to manufacturers to get the rights for production back home. I'm sure I'll find useful equipment we don't make in Australia as yet, or new products which may not even be on the market. For business initiatives, of course, local incentives must be right. I'm willing to devote my time and efforts, but if I can earn a better return by just leaving my capital in bank deposits my business enthusiasm may get dampened."

"Yes, that's what the book on economics says," Victoria nodded. "Capital and entrepreneurial initiatives are free agents; they move on if conditions become unattractive in one place. What remains is a backward standard of living."

Bernhardt saw another kindred thought in Victoria's comment. "To prevent this from happening, I've one more aspiration. I've run for Parliament before and I will do it again." Bernhardt's thoughts drifted off into the future, formulating ideas and plans.

Victoria looked at him with quiet esteem. "And what are some of your other ambitions?" she wondered after a while.

Bernhardt laughed, "You wouldn't believe it, but I am trying to become a better listener, trying to understand other people better. Just now, instead of doing that, we've been talking about me all the time. So tell me something of your life. What led you to the outstanding education you received?"

"Oh, that's a long story. We need not go into it."

Bernhardt put his hand over Victoria's. "We have plenty of time. In fact, we'll be in Burlington for days." They laughed. "This is the first time we've had an opportunity to talk to each other," Bernhardt mused. "I find it remarkable how our thoughts mingle and flow. So what skeletons do you have in your closet? Surely none in Australia. You arrived there only a few short years ago. So if anything, they must be back in England."

Victoria withdrew her hand slowly, reluctantly from under his. "You're right, there is some mystery. I don't know who my father is because I am illegitimate. He must've been of high standing. After I was born I believe he made a deal with my mother for his anonymity in return for setting up a generous trust for my education. The years before I went to the private boarding school I lived with my mother. I don't remember those years very well, but I know we lived in hardship."

"Perhaps we shouldn't go into it too much, if it troubles you," Bernhardt interrupted. "I don't want to spoil this time we have together here."

"No, it doesn't worry me much, but I know it has affected me. My mother wallowed in her misery. She chose me as the main reason for her melancholy. I also was her only audience when she complained about what a misfortune it was to have a child, and how it had ruined all her opportunities. Years of indoctrination must have succeeded with me. I still despise babies and toddlers. Isn't it amazing, children from the age I was when I left for boarding school I like well enough."

"You are very frank, Victoria, to admit this just as we have a new baby in the family. I'd be worried if I didn't know how well you have your emotions under control. But if you feel that way, isn't it odd to be a governess?"

"Well, there is little else I can do, and I love Sophia and Esther."

"What happened to your mother?"

"She died early. She really drank herself to death. Now I'll never find out who my father was. So, there you have it. I don't want children and that probably is one reason why I'm not married, since children are the natural consequence of marriage."

"Are there other reasons for such an attractive lady being unattached?"

"Well, I hate to say this," she smiled, "and present company excluded, but men in general don't like to settle with a well educated woman. They want to feel superior and in control. But I don't like being dominated. It brings out the worst in me."

Bernhardt laughed. "The devil in beautiful disguise, I'm sure."

"Yes, when I'm bad, I'm really bad."

"I can't believe that! You're just trying to keep me at bay again with your stories." Bernhardt shook his head and smiled. "I've heard a different version of what you've just said. 'When I'm good, I'm good, but when I'm bad, I'm really good!'"

Victoria couldn't help laughing.

"But of course, a proper young lady like you wouldn't know what I mean." He took her hand again and she held on to his.

"A real quandary," Victoria mused. "You know I admire you and I feel drawn towards you, but society stands between us. You are a married man with three children, a man of high standing with a peerless reputation. Your life has a purpose. There'd only be a lewd role for me here. I'm sure I'd relish it in the short term, but it'd have no future."

Bernhardt smiled sadly. "You've been sent as a devil to torture me. Your radiance alone sends my heart pumping whenever I see you, but now I also know the splendid spirit that lives behind your perplexing eyes. I'll be in continuous agony if I don't find a solution for this dilemma, Victoria."

"There is no solution. We'll both have to continue to suffer. I don't want to leave your household and be distant from you. Perhaps time will ease our heartache."

Governess and master took the carriage back to the hotel. For the short ride Victoria rested in Bernhardt's arms, feeling their bodies against each other. Back at the hotel, as they said goodnight to go to their separate rooms, Victoria was crying.

1877

EUROPE

Finally, the Holtermann travellers reached the high point of their journey, the Great Exhibition in Philadelphia. For days they took turns to see various sections of the world fair. They didn't have to queue as other visitors did. With special escorts they were whisked into the pavilions. The atmosphere was thrilling and cosmopolitan. Amazing novelties were shown, from the emerging phenomenon of electric technology to air ships and typewriting machines. Bernhardt's multitude of framed Australian pictures and grand panoramas was prominently displayed next to the stands of Canada, New Zealand, and Jamaica. Bernhardt and Harriet went to the Awards Ceremony. Competing with astounding displays from all nations of the world, 'Holtermann's Photographic Exhibit' was honoured with the coveted Bronze Medal. And then it was time to leave America.

In Hamburg, Bernhardt invited his relatives out to stylish traditional restaurants. Harriet and the girls could not speak with the family in German, so Victoria accompanied them as their translator.

"It is quite strange," Bernhardt commented to Harriet. "My old home town is not how I remembered it through all these years in Australia. It has grown and changed, but that is not the main difference. I had woven my whole childhood and youth into the memories of my home town. But my past is not here anymore. It is still good to see the historic streets and buildings, even the grimy harbour where I used to work."

Harriet nodded. "I'm impressed by the grand houses along the lake in the middle of the city. But the land is flat; only the front row gets a nice water view. It's not like Sydney with all its hills. Hamburg is wealthy and it's an elegant town, but I'm really excited about seeing London and Paris soon. And then we'll go through the new Suez Canal. How much we'll have to tell our friends when we get back home! I'm looking forward to being in Sydney again."

"Me too. But first I have to finish my presentations here. It'll take me across the country, even as far as Switzerland. I'm getting well back into speaking German again. It's important that I feel self-confident when I step in front of all these people, to be convinced of my own role and to be excited about what I have to offer. My pictures make that easy."

In Paris, Bernhardt and Harriet were busy again with the events and invitations related to the international exhibition. Victoria had time on her hands to visit the fascinating museums and galleries. She also practiced her French by reading the local papers. In one she came across an article written by a Parisian historian, writer and music critic by the name of Oscar Comettant who was on a visit to Australia, from where he sent reports about his impressions. Victoria enjoyed his story immensely and she set out to translate it into English to show it to the Holtermanns. She also intended to take it back to Sydney to see if it could be republished in a newspaper there. Or was Victoria simply enticed by the story because she was homesick for the distant town that had become her home?

'The drive through Sydney was very interesting, but I was impatient to visit the harbour, which, as everyone knows, is one of the marvels of nature. This drive, a feast for the eyes, was for me exquisite to the spirit also, for I had the good fortune to be accompanied by Monsieur le comte and Madame la comtesse de Sguier, who wanted to be my guides. I do not know the Bay of Constantinople, but I have seen the bays of Naples and Rio de Janeiro, and the comparison between these famous harbours, and that of Sydney, was not unfavourable to the latter. Madame la comtesse de Sguier showed me during the course of our drive how Sydney is built on a sort of peninsula in the form of a hand with spread fingers. This hand stretches out into the bay, and each finger is a promontory. This is why the streets running east-west in Sydney end in quays that are enlivened and jollied by ships whose masts sometimes rise above the height of the houses. I saw the harbour from a boat, but this is not enough to know it properly. Monsieur Paling, with kind alacrity, arrived next morning in his carriage to show me this wonder from above, looking down over ground dotted with flowers or the bare rocks that overhang and surround it. It was an unforgettable drive, the fairytale decor like a wonderful awakening dream transporting the imagination into a new world, exalting it and ravishing it with ecstasy. There are excellent shops, and even in America, the home of sumptuous hotels, I do not think there can be a finer establishment than the main hotel in Sydney. The stranger is surprised by the gigantic steam trams which serve the city and its environs; they are not elegant, these huge monsters, but they are certainly one of the curiosities of the city. Melbourne is more grandiose than Sydney, but Sydney has something more intimate about it, something, as it were, creole, and is therefore more attractive.

    Sydney's climate knows no winter and is cooled in summer by a sea breeze, and is thus remarkably healthy. In New South Wales, as in Victoria, one can breathe in the most comforting abundance of air. Today this large and admirable colony, whose resources of every sort are virtually incalculable, is marching rapidly towards the greatest possible prosperity, and its population is growing visibly from year to year.

Sydney has several theatres, museums, and libraries; there are a great number of schools, and also churches (the cathedral is really very beautiful), hospitals, etc., and an admirable zoo and botanical gardens. Government House (the governor's palace) is a monument to the Gothic style, dominating the bay and from a distance looking like a citadel. This palace contains some large and beautiful reception rooms, a very beautiful park, and the prettiest gardens in the world.

Only the total impossibility of prolonging my stay in Sydney could tear me away from all the attractions that conspired to keep me there. I would have liked to have piously saluted the memory of our great navigator, La Perouse, in front of the monument erected to his honour, in the form of a column on the capital of which is a bronze sphere. On the pedestal is the following inscription. 'This place, visited by Monsieur de La Perouse in 1788, is the last from which he sent news of himself.' The short time I spent in Sydney will never pass from my memory; it will remain as one of the most delightful pages in the book of my souvenirs, a page I shall often want to return to, and in which I shall re-read the very warm welcome extended me by Monsieur Paling and his family, and the no less cordial welcome I received from the members of the French Club, particularly Kowalski, the Wood family, Monsieur Conils, and Monsieur le comte and Madame la comtesse de Sguier. I shall see again, in memory, the rare curiosities in the unique museum that our French consul has created in his own house, and I shall hear the dear and highly expressive voice of the countess singing with other artists a whole collection of Spanish songs, some lively and staccato like a battery of castanets, others poetic, sombre and fatalistic, engendered by nostalgia for Granada after the fall of the last of the Abencerages. Ah! If this Spanish night in Sydney, following a dinner that was utterly French from the point of view of the wit of the guests, had been prolonged, I would certainly have missed my boat.

While still in Paris, Bernhardt managed to arrange another outing with Victoria, to a function Harriet didn't want to attend. All evening they were in the company of others, but on the walk back to the hotel Bernhardt and Victoria were finally alone.

The charming elegance and grandeur of the city and the exuberance of its inhabitants amplified the pair's romantic feelings.

"You're tormenting my heart and my mind," Bernhardt lamented, "knowing how we feel about each other, being constantly in your presence. Seeing your elegance, knowing your wit, looking at your exquisite body without being able to touch it. If we could only be together for one night. I've stood outside your door in a daze at night. I've touched your door knob and found the door locked."

"Yes, it'd be wonderful, but what difference would one night make? In these matters the brains of the smartest men fall between their legs. We must control our feelings. We need to think. How will it affect your family, and where will it leave me?"

"Yes, the family. I certainly did love Harriet and I still admire her. I wouldn't want to hurt her, but my feelings for you are so much stronger. I love you, Victoria."

They embraced in the balmy, fragrant air of a summer's night in Paris. They kissed with passion and couldn't let go of each other.

As they returned to the hotel Bernhardt's mind was spinning. "Tonight?" he asked.

"No, Bernhardt. I love you, too, but we can't, not like this. There are other things to life. What do you really want in the long term?"

"You are right, my love. I'll do anything to be with you, to be with you forever. Wait till we return to Sydney. We'll arrange things properly and realistically. I'll talk with my solicitor there and see what we can do. I love you, Victoria, with all my heart."

The great Paris *Exposition Universelle Internationale de 1878* drew to a close. It had attracted thirteen million visitors. Bernhardt's photographs were the main feature of the Australian pavilion. They were awarded a Silver Medal.

The overseas successes were diligently reported in the newspapers in Australia. There the *Sydney International Exhibition of 1879* was under preparation. In the Botanical Gardens in the centre of the city, sloping up from the harbour at Farm Cove, the grandiose Garden Palace was being constructed, featuring towers and a lofty central dome. After returning to Sydney, Bernhardt was able to devote an entire exhibition bay to the achievements of wetplate photography, profiling the works of Beaufoy Merlin and Charles Bayliss as well as his own. In Sydney, his exhibits won no prizes, but Bernhardt noted with satisfaction that many German entries received prizes, particularly in the categories of furniture and porcelain, pianos and other musical instruments.

1882

PARLIAMENT

At 674 George Street in Sydney a reception was held to officially launch the opening of Holtermann House, a new four storey commercial building. At hand was Holtermann's manager, William Slack, and a considerable number of representatives from the various wholesalers and retailers Bernhardt's company dealt with. Holtermann's office and warehousing staff were allowed to observe from the back.

A lectern had been placed beside a generously catered buffet. Mr Holtermann walked up to the lectern, addressing his guests, welcoming them and thanking them for their attendance.

"Here we are gathered," he continued, "to officially open our fine new business premises in this fashionable part of Sydney. In addition to our shops in Pitt Street and Liverpool Street, with this expansion we'll be better able to serve our distributors and customers. We will have room to handle the growth in merchandise and we are creating good working conditions for our employees."

He looked around the room.

"You are all familiar with the wide range we handle as Australian agents, but I would like to use this opportunity to mention some of our new products. As you know, on my trip around the world I was not only promoting Australia overseas, I also acquired a number of rights to act as agent. Some of the merchandise is arriving only now. One is the Davis Sewing Machine. We have already a few strong competitors in this area. That's why I intend to spend quite a bit of money on advertising, to support your sales efforts and to keep things moving. The sewing machine is of benefit mainly to the ladies, but I have also an exciting new product that caters more to men. We are now the first importers of German lager beer. We have just received a shipment from Munich, and you'll presently have the opportunity to sample its fine quality."

He paused to gather his thoughts before continuing with enthusiasm.

"Don't we live in the best of all times? Trade is flourishing around the world, we have peace and prosperity. Technology is advancing in leaps and bounds. There are already three hundred telephone lines in Sydney. In all of Australia we have now 4,000 miles of railway lines. Just last week I attended a banquet at the Wool Exchange where electricity generation was publicly demonstrated for the first time in our town. And already for three years we are using steamers with refrigerated chambers to send shiploads of hundreds of tons of beef, mutton and butter into the English market. I am still amazed about refrigeration! What an invention by our fellow Australian James Harrison. He stuck with it 'till it really worked. But we are shipping much other cargo, too, our ores and minerals, wool, wheat and tallow, pearl shells and the like. When I came to Sydney in the sixties there were a handfull of ship building companies here. Now we have over a hundred. Iron and brass foundries are stretched to their capacity, and so are machine shops, brick yards, saw mills and paint works. Our country is prospering and its cities are bursting at the seams."

He was interrupted by heart-felt cheers and applause from the audience.

"What I am particularly proud of is the local manufacturing I have been able to set up. We are now in full production of our gas producing equipment. And I am manufacturing our own telegraphic equipment in this country, equipment for which I see a bright future as more and more lines are being strung between distant places in this vast country. Telegraph offices looking like palaces are springing up in the big cities. We had already an undersea telegraph cable from here to New Zealand, but now the unbelievable has happened, we've a telegraphic connection from Australia all the way to Great Britain. We are well on the way to overcoming our sequestration from the rest of the world."

Mr Holtermann took a drink of water before he came to his conclusion.

"Finally, I would like to use this occasion to launch our new poster for one of our most advertised products, my 'Holtermann Life Preserving Drops'. As many of you may know I am convinced of the medicinal benefits of this product and I would like to give it the widest possible distribution for the welfare of its users. Since the image of the famous gold nugget with me standing beside it is well known in this country, we have decided to use it as a symbol for the Life Drops. Here then is the new poster."

Mr Holtermann revealed the placard showing his photograph and describing the many uses and benefits of the drops.

"Before I close, let me just mention one more thing which is not related to our business. You know I was nominated in the elections for the Legislative Assembly two years ago, and I lost badly. I had no hope against the sitting member, Farnell, who was also Secretary for Lands. But now that Farnell has left for New England and the population of our district has grown, I see a real chance of being elected. I want you to be among the first to know that I will run for Parliament again, and I am asking for your support."

The news elicited further applause and enthusiastic expressions of support.

"So, with all that good news out, I declare our new business premises officially opened. I am looking forward to many years of prosperous co-operation with you, our valued business partners, helped by my manager and by our dedicated staff. As long as we have each other's welfare in mind we will all be better off in the long term."

⚜

At the end of the day, back at his home, Bernhardt climbed to the top of the tower. The timber room which had served as a camera had long been removed. The stone railing and the corner spires remained. On the platform he encountered Victoria. She had taken the latest family addition, little Sydney, to watch the sunset. The sun had just disappeared below the horizon and was reflected in shades of pink and gold on small clouds in the west. The wooded hills lay dark, outlined by a purple rim. Below the hills the bays glistened in dark silver. Victoria's face was radiant in the twilight, mirroring the distant colours of the clouds. She put little Sydney down on a bench and embraced Bernhardt. They kissed tenderly.

Bernhardt inhaled the mild evening air deeply. He looked around and smiled. "Isn't it great to be back in Sydney, in this wonderful setting?"

Victoria kissed him again. She became contemplative. "How long will our bitter sweet love go on without a solution to our dilemma?"

"I think of you all day, my dearest. But there are so many obligations. Ever since we returned, I've been running in circles." It was true. Holtermann and Bill Slack worked long hours on the business deals the manager had delayed, waiting for Holtermann's return. The exhibition had to be set up in the Garden Palace and after that, works of art from the Sydney exhibition became part of the newly founded Art Gallery of New South Wales. In the midst of it all, the newest member of the family, son Sydney, was born. Holtermann was approached to take on more agency deals he had arranged overseas, which had led to his company becoming involved in manufacturing.

"But you enjoy all that," Victoria commented. "You thrive on industry and commerce, on your business deals and on your meetings with colleagues, staff and friends. At least I was able to help a little bit when all the crates arrived with the treasures we had bought during the two years of our journey around the world." She walked away to attend to little Sydney who had fallen asleep in the warm evening air.

"Yes, you did a marvellous job, Victoria. You fitted everything into the house so well, the paintings the sculptures, the tapestries, even all the bricabrac from so many countries. We wouldn't have found the time to do it with all the social engagements day and night. Everybody was so impressed. Now it is really our family home. What good taste you have, what sense of proportions. And you know me so well, Victoria, all my aims and passions. But you also should know that you are my greatest desire."

They leaned against the stone balustrade which was still radiating the stored heat of a sunny day.

"I don't doubt it, my dearest," Victoria nodded. "But I believe that there is no real hope for our love. To be honest, I'm thinking of leaving. It'll make it easier for both of us. We will get over the pain. We will have emptier lives, but without the conflict of endless yearning and hope."

Bernhardt grabbed Victoria's arm. "No, don't do that, Victoria, don't leave." He shook his head. "I'll find a way. I'll talk to my solicitor in confidence. He'll tell me what the options are, what I must do to finally live with you. We can't avoid hurting Harriet, but she'll be well off. Our love will persevere, Victoria. Destiny is what we make for ourselves and I'll make you mine. We'll lie together in sweet love."

They stood in a passionate embrace. Bernhardt's hands followed the outline of her slender body. Their kisses were full of lust. Soft darkness descended over the hills. A rim of deep red clouds still glowed in the west. The gas lights of the streets and squares of the city glimmered across the harbour.

⚜

Bernhardt had that private conversation with his solicitor. The advocate concealed his shock at Mr Holtermann's intentions. They discussed practical possibilities of how to implement them.

Victoria and Bernhardt met in the secluded garden pavilion near the water, the intricate metallic structure all overgrown with blossoming vines. He asked her to marry him. It would be a complicated and drawn out process, but their love would not be futile. Victoria accepted tearfully.

Late that night, after the family and all the servants had retired, the mansion called Holtermann Hall stood imposing and dark. As a distant thunderstorm was grumbling and flickering in the sky a faint light gleamed from one solitary window. It emanated from a candle in Victoria's bedroom. Bernhardt found the door unlocked. It would never be locked again.

⚜

Victoria was reading to Harriet from the newspapers again.

"Here is what the *Sydney Morning Herald* has to say," she announced pleasantly:

An Advertisement to the Electorate
Vote for Holtermann who has the courage to demand that your rights be accorded to you, your rights to the privileges of local opinion. Vote for Holtermann, and a judicious, but not indiscriminate immigration. Vote for Holtermann for free trade, free trade, free trade. Vote for Holtermann, who for the past ten years has given his earnest support to every public movement having for its object the advancement of your electorate. Holtermann and progress. Holtermann and local improvements. Holtermann and fearless representation. Holtermann for your vote."

Bernhardt entered the room carrying a notebook and pencil.

"Ah, our fearless leader," Harriet exclaimed. "We were just reading your campaign manifesto."

Victoria got up and excused herself but Harriet invited her to stay.

Bernhardt explained, "I'm jotting down notes for my campaign speech. I need more ideas for local improvements that I'll be able to propose to the House after I am elected." He sat down facing the two ladies. "Perhaps you can give me your suggestions on a few things we need here in the Northern region of Sydney? Still high on my list is a bridge spanning the harbour to replace the inadequate punts ferrying wagons and carriages across and to relieve the overcrowded steam ferries. Our northern area is prospering. We have sugar works and all sorts of industry here and we are even getting our own gas company at Neutral Bay now. But still, time might not be ripe yet for such a great project as a harbour bridge."

"You're right, Bernie," Harriet nodded. "It's better to think about proposals that can be achieved now."

"I still want to urge for increased immigration," Bernhardt insisted. "Not only migration of British subjects, but qualified people from other parts of Europe. I just read some figures from Germany. Last year 160,000 Germans moved to America, only 883 settled in Australia. It's easier and cheaper for them to go to America. With no direct shipping connection to Australia the costs are high. We are encouraging the British to come here by giving them a cheaper passage. We need to increase the financial advantages for other Europeans, too. They could embark at the harbour of Hamburg if a route can be arranged. And we have to increase government spending on advertising and public exhibitions overseas to get the right people interested."

"Yes, from Hamburg," Harriet commented, the memories flooding back, "what a nice city it is, with the Alster lake at its centre and its skyline of beautiful spires. The rich people live very well there, but I suppose for ordinary people it'd be much better here, particularly for people with ideas, with plans, and with determination to carry them through."

"Talking about shipping," Victoria suggested, "there is also room for improvement closer to home, here in Sydney. Since we won't have a bridge soon, we should at least have larger, government operated steam ferries running between the city and the North Shore, not just privately operated passenger and vehicle ferries. And the railway line could be extended down here from Hornsby to connect to the ferry."

"That's a good idea, Victoria," Harriet agreed.

Bernhardt scribbled in his notebook and nodded.

"And a tramway," Harriet continued. "That would make up the missing link, to carry ordinary people to and from work, to visit and to shop, to see their football and cricket on the weekends. And while we're at it we need a proper post office here on the north side, a respectable looking building."

"Excellent proposals," Bernhardt smiled. "They'll show people during the campaign that I'm on the right track. In the House I'll push government to implement changes that make it easy for commerce to grow which will increase prosperity for everybody."

"Water supply is another problem," Victoria remarked. "We are running low at times."

"Yes," Bernhardt agreed, "yet, there is plenty of rainfall that could be stored up in the Blue Mountains. A canal could be built from the Nepean River right to the city. Farmers could use it along the way for irrigation. I can see it could serve as a transport link and supply water for treatment in Sydney to become drinking water. I suppose the flow could be regulated to prevent flooding further down from the Nepean along the Hawkesbury River." Bernhardt hesitated. "I won't talk to you ladies about some of the unpleasantness being discharged into Port Jackson. But we must put a stop to that; we've got to keep our beaches clean. Now we have pumps. Large pumps are the solution, with extended ducts and sewerage tunnels."

"Plenty of good ideas are coming from this talk," Harriet smiled. "I hope you'll have enough support for them in the Assembly. Normally its just members pushing their own interests to benefit their own petty supporters."

"You are right," Bernhardt nodded. "With the exception of our would-be 'Father of Federation'."

"Ah yes, our good Premier of New South Wales, Sir Henry Parkes."

Bernhardt continued excitedly. "He has the larger picture in mind with his plan to set up a 'Federal Council of Australasia'. I'll certainly support his proposal for a meeting of delegates from all Australian governments, New Zealand and Fiji." Bernhardt's eyes glazed over in thought, anticipating future opportunities. Eventually he concluded with a grin, "I still have to be elected first. But I'm confident this time. It's my third attempt. Three's a good number."

As Bernhardt was getting up, Harriet reminded him of the arrangement she and Victoria had made for the day.

"Remember, we are taking the large carriage this afternoon to go to Manly with the children, to take a ride on the new ferry to the city."

"Ah yes, on the *Brighton*. I just talked with Mark Hammond about that ship, in the club recently. He is on the board of the Port Jackson Steamship Company that had her built in Scotland and delivered down here."

"She's the largest ferry we ever had," Harriet marvelled. "She can carry eleven hundred passengers."

"Yes, business seems to go well, from what Mark mentioned. Lots of people going on excursion to Manly now."

"They had to extend the wharf at Manly by fifty yards to accommodate the new ferry," Victoria mentioned.

"Well, have a nice outing together," Bernhardt smiled on his way to the door.

After lunch the nursemaid had the children dressed in sailor's uniforms and matching dresses. The driver had horses and carriage at the ready. Harriet and Victoria came down in their long dresses and fancy hats, exuding elegance. A footman was standing by. All climbed on board. The carriage wound its way through Mosman to the Spit, where it crossed Middle Harbour on a punt, climbed up the hill and finally descended towards the ocean panorama at Manly. They could see the big surf rolling in, turquoise and white. The driver turned right for the wharf on the tranquil Sydney Harbour.

There the *Brighton* was tied up, her decks overshadowing the wharf building. The sixty-seven meter steel hull gleamed darkly, with the wooden superstructure glinting in the sun. Two white chimneys up high and large paddle wheels on either side of the hull made her the pride of modern steam technology.

The Holtermann party made their way onto the polished wooden decking of the ferry. They passed the main saloon, handsomely fitted out with stained glass panels representing well known Scottish, English and Irish views. The group arrived in the Ladies Cabin. Harriet and Victoria were impressed by the carpeted floor and by the sofas and lounges in green and crimson velvet, with curtains to match around the large plate glass windows. The children ran to the silver cold water fountain to take drinks while the ladies checked their attire in gilt-framed mirrors along the walls.

"Silk curtains," Harriet remarked, "panelled and moulded ceilings, gilt cornices and trusses, and wood reliefs. Very nice."

"Isn't it remarkable how it all survived the rough journey from Scotland? Apparently they were caught in a bad storm. It ripped off some of the timber cladding protecting the saloons."

"Yes, and they burnt the rest of the cladding when they ran low on fuel."

"The ship looked strange with the temporary masts fitted

for the ocean voyage and with sails surrounding the chimneys. I saw a drawing in the paper."

As the party settled down, the slow, rhythmic movements of the mighty pistons and the revolutions of the big crank shaft in the centre of the hull started driving the wheels. The little harbour beach at Manly was soon behind. They passed the tall cliffs of The Heads. The swell running in from the open sea rolled the ship gently from side to side. The captain turned starboard for the centre of Sydney. Wooded green hills along the route provided pleasurable vistas through the windows.

"Don't we live in the best of all times?" Harriet said to Victoria. "The world is at peace, commerce is thriving, people see opportunities for their advancement and prosperity all around us." Harriet watched her children tease each other. "And my family is well and happy. The gods have smiled on us."

1885

LAST BIRTHDAY

Bernhardt was in Victoria's bedroom. Victoria, beautiful in her elaborate dress, sat on the bed sobbing.

"First it was the election campaign," she recalled resentfully. "I can understand that you didn't go ahead with the divorce then. But after you'd won your seat there was nothing to prevent you then."

Bernhardt put his hand on her shoulder. "Harriet was expecting Leonard," he explained. "I'd have been ready to act, but that was not the right time. Little Leonard got in the way."

Victoria raised her voice and pushed him away. "Ah, you and your babies. Nothing but trouble, that's what they are. Leonard is more than one now and you're into your second year in Parliament."

Bernhardt's halting voice did not reflect the self-aggrandisment of his reply. "I am a pillar of the community now, with a reputation I need to maintain and to preserve for future generations to remember."

"You've long been a respected man. When you said you'd get a divorce to marry me you were already running for Parliament. You never meant it," Victoria yelled. "You've deceived me. All you wanted was a convenient mistress, not a new wife."

"I have always been in love with you," Bernhardt pleaded. "I was aching to be with you. I meant what I said, but now I feel so deeply tired and apathetic. I am not the man I used to be. I am sick."

"You don't look sick. You have no fever. It's just another excuse, Bernhardt." He supported himself on the dressing table and closed his eyes, unable to reply. Victoria calmed down. "So I'll have to resign myself to the fact that it'll never happen. That's obvious."

Bernhardt forced himself to regain his posture. "Victoria, believe me, I still have the most tender feelings for you." He walked to the window and looked down at the pavilion in the splendour of the summer garden. "I've seen the solicitor and I've included you in my will. You are much younger than I am. You'll certainly benefit from it. At least in this form I'll be with you for the rest of your life, even after my death."

⚜

Victoria went to see Charles Bayliss in the photographic studio at the back of the house.

"Good to see you," he smiled. "Are you ready to sit for the portraits now? We must preserve Australia's beauty in all its forms, not just landscapes and cities. I will be very honoured, if you can find the time."

"Thanks for the compliment. Well, would the walking dress I am wearing be the type of attire you want to photograph?"

"We can start with that, and we could add something more elaborate later, perhaps a visiting dress."

Victoria changed the subject. "I heard you'll set up your own studio in Sydney soon."

"Yes, with Mr Holtermann's help I have found a good shop in the city. I'll actually start moving some of the equipment today. Hunt is coming to help me."

"Hunt, you say? Is that the miner from Hill End?"

"Yes, that's the one."

"Mr Holtermann has talked about him. They go back a long time together."

"The chief doesn't seem to like him for some reason. Slack told me that Hunt had asked for work around the house here. When Slack mentioned it to Holtermann he was adamant that he not be given a job. He said he had been warned about Hunt."

"Warned? About what?"

"I have no idea. Anyway, Slack asked me if Hunt could help me, for old times sake. That's why he is coming here today."

Victoria looked around the room. "What's in all the bottles on the shelves here, Charles?"

"Oh, these are the chemicals for producing wetplate negatives, for development, fixing and so on."

"You are so clever with all that chemistry. I've heard that some of the substances you are using are poisonous. With which ones do you have to be most careful?"

"I guess the worst is this one here, potassium cyanide. Working with it for years probably led to Merlin's early death. And now I understand Mr Holtermann has similar symptoms. I'm younger, but I have been warned to get out of this profession."

"Really, who says so?"

"Mr Holtermann's physician. He came to have a look at the chemicals here. Did the doctor tell you about our chief, too?"

"No, I had no idea Mr Holtermann might be affected."

"Oops, perhaps I shouldn't have said anything. The doctor said not to let on to the family, so please be discreet."

Outside the studio, Hunt had approached quietly and stood out of sight near the open door, overhearing the end of the conversation.

"All right, Charles," Victoria was saying. "For my portrait should I wear an elegant dinner dress then? And fix my hair better? I'll come back when I've had time to prepare myself."

Hunt knocked at the door and walked in. Charles introduced him to the governess. They exchanged a few pleasantries. Then Victoria left.

After she had seen the carriage with Charles and Hunt depart, she returned to the studio with a small flask. Carefully she transferred some of the potassium cyanide and took it to her room. She opened a little bottle of Holtermann's Life Preserving Drops and replaced a small part of its contents with the poisonous chemical. She knew Bernhardt always had one of the bottles on his bedside table and took a few drops religiously at least twice a day.

Bernhardt had not wanted a party for his birthday as he had not felt well lately. Nevertheless, Harriet had sent word to a few friends to partake in five o'clock tea at Holtermann Hall that day. While Bernhardt was still resting, the wellwishers arrived and were shown in to the huge drawing room. On this mild autumn day at the end of April, the doors were open to the terrace overlooking the Holtermann property, eight acres of green parkland in brilliant sunshine and warm shadows.

Bernhardt came down to join the guests. As he entered the room, he thought how familiar the setting had become to him over the years, but he marvelled again at its beauty, the high walls in powerful, deep colours, the patterned ceiling with intricate cornices, prodigiously heavy curtains, the many paintings in massive frames, ornate, heavy furniture, rare carpets, ivory and silver ornaments and fine porcelain everywhere. Bernhardt knew one day soon he would have to leave all this. He was moved at seeing the gathering of family and friends. How often would he still be able to greet them?

The silent footmen in their horizontally striped waistcoats were offering tea and crumpets, supplemented by Scotch whisky, port, tokay, madeira, sherry, and champagne along with a generous variety of hors d'oeuvres.

Bernhardt was elegantly dressed in a black frock coat cut to uniform length above the knee. He wore grey trousers. His shirt was fine linen muslin. With white gloves he held a luxuriously carved cane, inlaid with mother of pearl. Despite being as well groomed as ever, he looked grey and haggard as he slowly made his way around the room to shake hands with his guests and accept their birthday wishes. As he reached the great staircase at the end of the room, he went up a few steps. Leaning on his cane he raised an arm for attention to address the small gathering.

"Dear family, dear friends, isn't it amazing that today is the exact anniversary of the day I arrived here in Australia? Today I turn 47. I still can picture myself walking off the boat into an exciting new world on my 20th birthday. I remember discovering Sydneytown in its lush setting, so graced by nature, making me feel privileged to have arrived here. The town with its self-confident bustle didn't seem to know it was located at the far end of the world. Hill End was even further afield, many days on foot through the plains, the mountains and the bush. But once you were there, you got captivated by the entrepreneurial spirit and fascinated by the lure of gold. The long hours down the lonely mine shafts may have flowed like molasses, but the years went by in a flash. What a rollercoaster ride it has been!" He shook his head and smiled. "Whatever happens, even if the journey ends in black oblivion, we still can enjoy the thrill of the ride! I had my ups and downs to equal any man. When you start with nothing, like I did, you expect things can only get better. But I had to learn that still it always can get worse. Harriet and I went through bleakest of desperation. Not in my wildest dreams could I have imagined then that I would stand here today in all this grandeur!"

"Hear, hear," came the cheers from the gathering, applauding Bernhardt's achievement.

"I'm very happy to have with me today quite a few of you who played an important part in my life's journey. Some of us met in Sydney in those early days. My dear Harriet, who has stayed with me through all our trials and tribulations.

Her wonderful parents, at whose house in Bathurst a certain out-of-luck miner always found a place at the table. As the saying goes, behind every successful man stands a supporting wife and a very surprised mother-in-law."

Spontaneous laughter erupted, even though the general mood was not so jovial. It was obvious to all that Bernhardt was not well. But he continued his address undeterred.

"I am particularly pleased to see Mary and Louis here today after a long absence. It was Louis who urged me to try my luck at goldmining and we stuck it out together for many years 'till we succeeded. There is another person here to whom I owe much in this regard, my old friend Mark Hammond. We've had our disagreements, but he followed his conviction, and I'm glad he did. Mark is now mayor of the Sydney suburb of Ashfield, which is particularly prospering since the new railway line has a station there, and Mark is also an honorable colleague of mine in Parliament."

There were more cheers and applause. Bernhardt's mind flashed back to Hill End, to a chilly morning, to a group of angry men standing in the rubble at the top of the mine shaft. He felt his hot hand on the cold handle of his knife as he lurched forward towards his adversary. That was his darkest hour in a time of desperation. Hill End, how far back it lies, he thought, like in another life. Bernhardt let his eyes wander over the elegant group in the mansion and smiled.

"I would like to thank our friends from around Sydney for coming here to help me celebrate. And I am very happy to welcome my brother, and my friend Chan, once also of Hill End, now a successful merchant in our prosperous city. And there are others who we met later on and who have become very dear to us. I would like to mention our governess, Victoria, who plays such an important part in our large household and who passes on her wisdom and her common sense to our five beloved children."

It might have sounded peculiar to the guests that Bernhardt alluded to the governess, unless they considered the two year journey around the world Victoria had taken with the family. That must have brought her very close to Bernhardt and Harriet. Bernhardt averted his eyes from Victoria who stood with some of the children. Her graceful figure was enhanced by an elegant blue tea gown. He continued, talking slowly.

"Yes, wisdom. That makes me think of what is important in life. It is not financial success. That is only a measure of one limited aspect of our endeavours. We won't be happy unless our lives are fulfilled in other areas besides rewarding work. I am blessed with a devoted wife and a cheerful band of children. My life is enriched by friends and loyal associates. I am truly grateful for all your support. But there are two more things we need to round out our lives."

Bernhardt paused again. Then he seemed to recover strength from the spirit of his philosophy.

"Living means changing and to be ready for change, to conquer our fear of the unknown, to challenge our mental faculties with new endeavours, to stretch our mind and our emotional boundaries. Life is either an exciting adventure, or nothing at all!"

"Hear, hear," the audience called. "Bravo!"

The listeners were pleased to have found another reason to cheer. Bernhardt gathered his thoughts. He remembered how self-centred and narrow-minded he had been as a young man, always considering what others could do for him, charming them to his advantage, helping others only in expectation of ample credit for his deeds, not aiming to be of generous service to the world around him. What a short-sighted approach, he thought, how egotistical and uncaring. How long it had taken him to grasp the full picture, to see himself only as a small knot in the large net of people around him. In such a wider frame of mind he had found a lasting sense of direction for his own life, a purpose for his existence. With this thought he continued his address.

"In essence, to lead a full life we need a purpose larger than ourselves, a road to travel without ever reaching its end. We need a mission that touches others, that leaves a legacy. What we put into our own life is lost when we die, but what we put into the lives of others continues to live on. I was lucky to have found such challenges and to have pursued them with vigour, be it in promoting our graceful country to the world, be it in enhancing its growth and prosperity with my new business ventures, or be it in Parliament, where much still remains to be done."

He raised his arm in a wide gesture. "In this vein, let me conclude with a few words as a politician. Don't we live in a magnificent world these days? The nations live in peace and balance. Britain, Germany, France, America, the Austro-Hungarian Empire, the Russian Czardom, all strong and prosperous countries, trading with each other, developing their colonies. This is what we need, free and open access for worldwide commerce. Technology is advancing, we live in a world of change and growth. No country can hide behind barriers designed to keep out competition. Such a country would only fall behind in efficiency and in industrial development, it would weaken, and its standard of living would not hold pace with the world."

Bernhardt cleared his throat. As he continued in a stronger voice he shook his head.

"Isn't it amazing how Karl Marx is now gaining popularity with his Communist ideology. He had made waves in Germany already before I left there. And he joined forces with Engels in London. Socialism is now regarded as a science!" Bernhardt laughed. "Don't these people see that it is a utopian dream? It won't work, human nature is not so altruistic. If applied, such ideals would only be perverted and do more harm then good. But I have faith in Australia. The people here are realistic and have the right sense of balance. Here we are living in a country blessed with rich farmland, fishing grounds, tropical gardens, endowed with coal, ores and minerals, gold and precious stones. But we cannot rest on our luck, and we cannot escape the world we live in. If other countries can produce things cheaper we'll lose investments and our people will lose their jobs. There's no god-given right to a good job. If we don't find an ideal position, we have to take a rough one. I've done it for many years in my life. Our country needs to remain lean and efficient. We can only afford a limited bureaucracy and only a judicious level of government subsidies. If politicians squander our money and raise taxes, business and employment will go overseas."

"Hear, hear," came the calls of approval from some of the listeners.

"But I'm not in Parliament here. We are among family and friends. And I am getting tired of speaking. Let me come to a conclusion."

Bernhardt felt feeble. Mentioning far away countries reminded him of the fair places he had seen in America, in Europe, and here back home. What a beautiful world, he thought.

How ingeniously people were developing and prospering everywhere. What a marvellous time to live in. So much that still remained to be done. But who had finished more in a lifetime than he had? Not many.

"In conclusion, I would like to give a final word of advice to my children. Rely on yourself, not on institutions, companies, government. Find your own purpose in life, concentrate on your own aims, work and play with like-minded reasonable people. Above all, give and share, don't demand. This'll make you happy."

Bernhardt bowed slightly to the clapping and the calls of approval. He smiled with thin pale lips. He felt weak and fatigued, but as he looked around the room at his family and friends he knew they were the gold he had been dreaming about since childhood. Observing them now gave him that feeling of joy and wholesome fulfillment emanating from his stomach and rising to his chest. Bernhardt retained that emotion as he stepped down and chatted with a few of the guests. But soon he was too tired.

"Enjoy yourselves in each other's company," he said after a while. "I must rest. Harriet will look after you."

He kissed Harriet briefly and looked at the children on his way to the stairs. How blessed I am, he thought. His feeling of warmth and joy rose again. Victoria was standing near the bottom of the landing. She excused herself from the children and helped Bernhardt up the stairs. As they walked slowly together, Bernhardt saw a picture in his mind's eye of Victoria sitting opposite him in the restaurant in America, telling him about her childhood, listening to him about his dreams and aspirations. Again he felt her body resting against his side as during the carriage ride back to the hotel in America. What a moment of adoration and longing it had been.

In the spacious bedroom in Holtermann Hall, Victoria took Bernhardt's coat and eased him down onto the bed.

"My Life Drops," he said, reaching over and taking a sip from the little bottle.

Bernhardt lay on his back and closed his eyes. He felt Victoria taking his hand. Did he have any regrets, he pondered. No. He had not wasted the time that had been given to him. He had not taken the obvious and the easy path. He had forged an idea of his principal aims, and he had pursued them in inventive ways. Small regrets, perhaps. He should have gone to the beach more often as he grew older. Swimming is such a pleasure, leisurely strokes in a calm bay, sensing the water swirling around your limbs, feeling part of the beauty of nature around you. Bernhardt saw himself as a little boy, splashing in the shallow water of a lake. He ran ashore to his father, who took him by the hand for a walk under the tall trees. Papa lifted him up towards the sky and placed him on his shoulders. Little Bernhardt rode like a giant close to the branches of the trees from light into shadow into light into shadow into darkness.

The physician had been sent for. Harriet and Victoria went upstairs with him. Bernhardt's eyes were closed. After a brief examination the physician turned around.

"The honourable Mr Holtermann is dead," he said.

Harriet sat down on the bed, took Bernhardt's hand and cried.

Victoria went to her room, opened a drawer and took out the bottle of poisoned Life Preserving Drops. At the open window she removed the stopper, pouring the contents down into a bed of flowers. The poisoned drops had never been used.

Holtermann Park stood like a lush painting of huge trees, of lawns, shrubs and flowers sloping down to the water, framing a view across the harbour to the multitude of tall ships before the solid buildings of the city. Victoria stayed at the window. Through her tears she looked down to the garden pavilion.

At the grand funeral for Mr Holtermann, Mark Hammond, Mayor of Ashfield and Member of Parliament, delivered a speech. He started in a quiet voice:

"Today we say an untimely early farewell to Bernhardt Holtermann, father of five children, a great family man, a great friend, and one of the greatest businessmen of Australia. I have known Bernhardt for practically all the years he spent here in this country, from our mining days as partners at Hill End, to being colleagues in Parliament here in Sydney. But more than partners and colleagues, we were true mates and friends. This privileged position gave me an understanding of Bernhardt's spirit, of his aspirations from early on in life. What made him special was that he had a vision for his life. From the time when he was a young man in his native Germany, he wanted three things: He wanted to be independent, entrepreneurial and artistic. Bernhardt realised that he could not achieve his dreams back in Hamburg, given his humble background and the rigid society he lived in. He collected all his courage and sailed the incredible distance to his unknown land of hope, to Australia. Here, as we all know, he pursued his vision with incredible determination, but also with flexibility when it was called for. And he was most co-operative, socially, in business, and in his family life."

Mark Hammond let his eyes wander over the congregation before he continued with emphasis.

"Bernhardt has achieved all of his life's goals –to be independent, entrepreneurial and artistic. He certainly became independent as soon as he hit these strange shores here down under. He accepted full responsibility for his life, regardless of his background, his handicaps and his setbacks. He gave himself no excuses. Secondly, Bernhardt Holtermann became entrepreneurial, initially by staking out a claim together with Louis Beyers, then by making the mine public on the stock market, and finally in a big way by setting up his many prosperous enterprises in trading and in manufacturing. Finally, Bernhardt was able to pursue his third dream, to express his artistic talents. He did this in the most modern form available in our times by using the art of photography, which he advanced to new horizons and to a grandeur which gained him world-wide recognition."

Mark Hammond glanced briefly at his notes before he continued in a slow and strong voice.

"Let me conclude by thanking Bernhardt Holtermann for what he has given to us and to the world. For not only has he fulfilled his life's vision, Bernhardt has left a legacy. He will continue to live in his family, in the heart of his wife Harriet, and in the minds and bodies of his five beautiful children, and in their children to follow. This family is one of the cornerstones of our prosperous society with its splendid household and its towering mansion. Furthermore, Bernhardt has given this country his thriving business enterprises, which will provide employment and commercial impetus for the years to come. In Parliament he has advanced legislation supporting economic development and worldwide trade. And finally, Bernhardt has given us the legacy of his immense photographic records. They will endure as well and show future generations how we lived, what we built and how we expanded the foundations for the glorious development of our beloved country. Bernhardt Holtermann, we bow before you and thank you for the bequest you left in our hearts and for the legacy you left to our country."

Many months later, as the Holtermann household was preparing to vacate the mansion on the hill to move to less ostentatious quarters, Victoria received a letter from Mr Edwards in London. He mentioned that he had heard of Mr Holtermann's death and he recalled the visit of the Holtermann family to London, when he had met Victoria and had had the opportunity to spend some time with her. Finally, he made her a proposal of marriage. He offered to send her a ticket for the voyage to London, where, after a suitable period of courtship, they could be wed.

Victoria had by now reconciled herself to Bernhardt's death. Four of the children in her care already went to school and little Leonard would follow soon. Victoria had fond memories of Mr Edwards as a true gentleman. Before making up her mind, she discussed the prospect with Mrs Holtermann.

"Of course, you'll go, Victoria! What an excellent man, Edwards. It will be hard for me and the children, but we can't stand in your way. You must go!"

Victoria agreed, "Yes, I shall." For the first time ever, Harriet put her arms around Victoria and the two ladies stood in silent embrace.

The wedding took place in London the following year.

Edwards was grateful he had met Victoria through Bernhardt. Through the bliss Victoria brought into Edwards' life, Bernhardt Holtermann unwittingly repaid his old miner's debt to Edwards.

Hunt was still roaming the streets and alleys of London. He had developed an unshakable drinking habit which he supported with petty crime and begging, even with a spot of work at times. One day he collected enough courage to make his way to Edwards' house in the West End to ask once more for his pay off. Victoria was just on her way out the door and met him as he approached. Seeing her in London, Hunt realised he would no longer have any chance with his opportunistic claim. After Victoria had recognised Hunt again, she inquired about his situation. From his rambling reply she could glean enough information to conclude that the old gold digger had lost his way and that there was nothing she could do to help him. Hunt left abruptly. That was the last Victoria ever saw or heard of him.

Four years after Bernhardt's death, Victoria received the news that the mansion in North Sydney, Holtermann Tower as it was called by then, had been sold to the Sydney Church of England Grammar School. It was a prestigious private school for boys, more practically and jovially referred to as 'Shore'. Victoria was pleased. After the lavish dinners and receptions the house had seen, after the extravagant family lifestyle it had supported, after the grand photographs taken from its tower, and after the love and the heartbreak the manor had witnessed, it was her own profession of teaching within those walls that would endure in the form of an elite school.

Thus far, with rough and all unable pen,
our bending author has pursued the story,
in little room confining mighty men,
mangling by starts the full course of their glory.
Small time, but in that small, most greatly lived ...

William Shakespeare

Epilogue

It was a great delight to hear that Gunter Schaule was to write a novel depicting the life and times of my great grandfather Bernhardt Otto Holtermann.

The only accounts I had of him were what I had read, some derogatory. The way Gunter has portrayed Holtermann reflects the family pride of my father and my grandfather Leonard Holtermann. People who knew our family always spoke of my great grandfather and grandfather as gentlemen.

Bernhardt Otto Holtermann has always been an inspiration to me. My first recollection of him was a grand oil painting at the top of the landing in my grandparents' home in Chatswood. The portrait was larger than life, exactly a true account of the man.

My grandfather never really knew his father. Leonard was a man of property and lived his life on his estate in Chatswood, where he later cared for his elder sister, Sophia, in her old age. Leonard won many awards at the Royal Easter Show. In the 1930s, Len, as he was known to his friends, was kicked by a horse and never recovered. He was an invalid for many years and died at the age of 60 from Parkinson's disease. My father was his only descendant.

As much as Len retained the wealth he inherited which provided his livelihood, my father was different. My father worked as a motor mechanic. He was very knowledgeable and intelligent. He tried his hand at business. After inheriting the family fortune, things changed. He had a fire pile that went for weeks, destroying the history his father had preciously kept during his lifetime. Within a year of inheriting his parents' home he sold the property. He then moved into another property he had inherited in Mosman. We lived there for nine years before that was sold and we moved to another inherited property on the waterfront on Pittwater. My father lived out his life there, working on motor boats up to the time of his death at age 75.

I often think how long are we here? Indeed why are we here? Is it all beer and skittles? Do we have a purpose to this life? Is our purpose just to work, rear a family and die? Or is there more? We all know life is a struggle!

The late Bernhardt Otto Holtermann was a remarkable man and his life showed what a large factor in success is a longterm vision, and indomitable perseverance, a quality he possessed in an unusual degree. He stuck to the mining claims with unflagging endurance for many years. Mr Holtermann also prided himself on being an Australian, recognising to the full extent the advantages he enjoyed as an Australian. Holtermann's gold was not only the gold that was extracted at Hill End. The real gold was the legacy he left future Australians, a history in photography that really is priceless. He took what he had and he used it. His life was a lesson in doing and in giving.

Let me plant some seeds in your mind to achieving what you want in life. Firstly you must have a vision of what you hope to achieve. Have you discovered what your nugget is? Second you must have the courage to act. To persevere, to plan, the boldness to get out on the limb, show your hand, forget what others will think. If you really believe, you will achieve. Lastly, you must have faith. Without faith you are a ship without a rudder. You must have faith in yourself, faith in this great country, and faith in your God.

John Holterman